Dan River Anthology, 1986

Edited by

Richard S. Danbury III

*To June Purdom —
my dear friend. Thanks
for opening the door.
Love,
Vera Lee Baker*

ISBN-0-89754-045-X

Dan River Press
South Thomaston, Maine U.S.A.

Contents

To tomorrow

Carol Adler
Pittsford, NY

Dear Friends

Once again it's time
to share with you
what's new here well
Mary is well again
if you remember about this time
last year as soon as we'd got
the Xmas tree up and the
icicles on she developed a severe
intolerance of sex and
food but all that has passed and
we are once again enjoying
our vegetable garden

although as a result
the dog contracted syphillis
and died.

Egypt was nice in last month's
NATIONAL GEOGRAPHIC especially King
Tut's Tomb in color on page 52
although the slides we got last summer
had a better angle

and Mary's Aunt Louise
sent us some huckleberry jam but
it broke before it came
Gerald is fine he is still
growing and our neighbor
Bob Black
bought a boat but we haven't been
in it yet
because of the snow.

In June Steffanie
got her PhD but the plumbing
broke in the middle of
convocation so we never did
see her process since there was
water everywhere and the auditorium
was quite a mess by the end
it seems like it was a
faulty toilet in the Men's
Room

she doesn't have a job yet
but she's hoping and anyway
she loves to cook and the cat
keeps her busy.

When the Fall came
we knew it would be early
even though one is never
quite prepared and much of the time
Jim was up to his neck in fighting off a
bad case of grippe that took its
toll we heard although
I was lucky and we only missed
the annual clambake that was
cancelled anyway.

For my birthday the twins
sent me around the world
in addition to a new nightgown
and I'm looking forward to
putting it on when they
come for New Year's they said
if the car is fixed in time

and if Lucky gets her
days off so they don't
have to rush back they are
both busy but fine
and we couldn't ask for a
greater blessing.

So to conclude
we're hoping Cindy's baby
will be a boy but we'll
take anything since she's having it
naturally. We'll let you know
probably next year at this time
meanwhile may it be a peaceful
season so we can hear from you soon
and remember our number is still
outside and in the book only
Pa's has changed and if you like
pudding I made a double batch
this year and more stars than
usual for the people across
the street who just moved in
the house was empty for
so long

Mary Jim Gerald Steffanie Ma Pa Mindy Sandy and Cindy Todd
Ted Fido Rusty Skipper Baby Bobby and Spot

P. S. Tammy and Dick moved into a new house
        that's the color of dog shit
        but they plan to redo it.

Anneke Mason
Tacoma, WA

The Hunt

Between the Maoris' sticks and Mondriaan's
squares we lived thousands of years
Deer and stick were revered
No magic doubted within their lines
For spirits past and present lived
within the caves, guided the artist's
hands and eye when in shadows of ancient
trees wild creatures quenched their thirst
and the sharpened stone would pierce
to send all others on mad flight

Accepted their due in shares of flesh
and blood, watched hunter turn hunted,
young warriors impale themselves
on mammoths' tusks
For they were relentless and demanding,
easily angered and difficult to appease
They spoke in the thunder and buried
their victims in flowing lava
They were understood and man paid respect,
drew and carved to implore his Gods
under the roof of his ancestors
His art was everyone's

Clean lines of Alta Mira Caves
done in three dimensions now
I stand before Picasso and recognize---
From somewhere in my past, fear overcomes
And spirits speak, their voices shrill,
penetrate the marrow of my bones, foretell---
And fire once more erupts, quenches
appetites of Gods, buries once more

4

Anneke Mason
con't

the living in ashes
The artist captures the bull and halts
his brainless lurches, pins him down
between the haunted---Implores!
But only he and I have understood

Ann Wallin
Green Valley, AZ

Protrait Of China - 1923

One morning, riding in a rickshaw
Down Nanking Road in Shanghai,
I watched six coolies
struggling, single-file,
A rope stretched tight
Across their backs and shoulders,
Their faces grim and twisted,
Slowly pulling
A great load of heavy broken rocks
On a protesting two-wheeled cart.
And hanging on the rope
Between two of the straining men
There was a bird-cage.

And the bird was singing.

Marijane G. Ricketts
Kensington, MD

Arenas International

In sinew tensed to ripples,
power ploys official
flick off political flies
from hips omnipotent.
And turncoats
lift their sticky feet
from flypapers judicial
in Washingtons of the World.

Would-be heads of state
who crumble the names of contenders
over executive linens,
whose senses blunt obliquely,
no longer can ignore
the world's ignoble faces —
for the camera frames its pawns
in Washingtons of the World.

Everyone pays for the laundering
of linens presidential.
In Earth's beleaguered palaces,
we work the globe wheel round
its bumpy spindle,
unrequited still
to shudders of a shrinking planet
and potentates upper-residential
in Washingtons of the World.

Nita Bourbon
Dallas, TX

At Home Alone

the house creaks and
moans its complaints

outside a tree scratches
objections on the window

shadow creatures scurry
around the dark corners

of my mind

silence becomes solitude
yet ceases to be solace

atmosphere hangs
heavy with time

while morning waits
to fondle the night

before slipping
in wet with dew

Annette S. Crouch
Lancaster, CA

Ballerina

Dance is love
in physical emotion
flowing from my skin
taking control
moving me with song

My feet know
without my mind telling
Dance is a breath
of life exposed

In and out and in and
Out of my body I dream
Dancing on the winds
of time I fly free

To step like a *prima donna*
onto the stage of life
Twirling in cadence
Breathing the stage lights
Embracing the song.

Jeanne Shannon
Albuquerque, NM

From A Painting Of The Annunciation

On a green morning in the Mediterranean spring
Gabriel and the Archangel, bearer of messages,
drifted through blossomy skies,
past islands of jade and parchment.

The woman stood by the doorway,
under a budding elder tree,
gathering herbs for the evening table:
fennel and dill and fenugreek.

Rubies crackled in the pavement;
the sun gave forth a purple light.

     "Our Lady of the Rubies,
      Our Lady of the Elder Tree. . ."

The herbs fell from her hands.

He gathered them up and offered them to her,
then floated upward, over the western gate,
his great gold wings beating the air.

The elder tree was in full flower. . .
and violet evening fell.

Linda Back McKay
Minneapolis, MN

Katie

In hog heaven
with comic books
and sweet tarts
sprawled on an armchair perch
far from Korea,
hunger, abandonment, pneumonia
high on oblivion
and sweet tarts
deep in Incredible Hulk,
G.I. Joe, Voltron
muscled fighters
bully beaters
Katie tenacious treasure
sensitive as a hang nail
odd as a stray sock
Katie a butterfly cupped in my hand
wants me to tell her that growing up
is child's play.

Mary Engel
North Bergen, NJ

The Grass Is Greener In Scarsdale

cracked sidewalks/tenements with body odor
Noah's stray dogs with rabies
horses they shot in daylight
suppertime parents sang arias from open windows
I grew up ignorant
mother said storks bring babies
Winnie my tree of knowledge
her father a porter on the choo-choo train
slipped in and out of town like a shoehorn
Izzy played with dolls at forty
dancing between the garbage cans
Strauss waltzes throbbing in the cretin brain
Anna in the railroad flat with her newborn
phantom husband hounded by the cops
death played marbles/skipped rope/rode a pony
Stella reaching for a doll she drops
falls five stories from the fire-escape
Alonzo in the bedroom with the beaded portieres
face like a peeled apple/too late for a mother's tears
America at war
soldiers flowing past like ticker tape
neighbors with sons/Germans who were kin
growing up with the Charleston and bathtub gin
not knowing I was poor
not knowing I was Jewish
unitl someone branded me with the Star of David

Karren L. Alenier
Chevy Chase, MD

Chuy Gives Me A Souvenir

in the kitchen
my sister serving
tequilla and salt
Chuy handing me 500 pesos
his boots firm on the floor
we talked about the day in Nuevo Laredo
bargaining on the street
we talked about the ride out in the brush
my son between two men —
Tio and Uncle
excited as jack rabbit
excited as jack rabbit
Tio and Uncle
my son between two men
we talked about the ride out in the brush
bargaining on the street
we talked about the day in Nuevo Laredo
his boots firm on the floor
Chuy handing me 500 pesos
tequilla and salt
my sister serving
in the kitchen

Nina LaGrassa
Forest Hills, NY

The Door Ajar

A room away, a lifetime away
The door remains ajar
Never closed, but never fully opened.
Entrances are stymied
Precluding the pain of exits.
Tenaciously, the door remains ajar
A bulwark against seperation,
A promise of potentiality,
A bridge, a barricade.
Sometimes, a fleeting glance
In, out or through the door
Provides a momentary connection,
A tentative bond, but
The lives on either side of the door
Shroud themselves in anonymity,
Protecting themselves from the pain of love and loss,
Shielding themselves from the magic
Of total intimacy.

M. McNeil
Brooklyn, NY

Adirondack Pond

To have a body of water myself
freshly fed, warmed by a spring of sun
I doubt I should ever leave the forest.

Especially dark hours when the moon
rises a sliver short—bullfrogs muscle
low notes to the edges, and from cold depths
large trout jump.

— ★ —

M. McNeil
Brooklyn, NY

Land Of Gods

It is twilight in the land of gods.
Grand white temples line a runway of spring lawn.
In blooming trees old kites flicker, and close to the soul
Lincoln's pool is calm:

reflected is the garden of America
the balm and hush of night adored.

Rabiul Hasan
Lorman, MS

On An Indian Reservation In Central Mississippi

1.
Outside the gravelled main street of mucky tenements,
A Choctaw Indian girl licks an ice cream cone happily
Before Big Joe's Grocery in Philadelphia, Mississippi.

2.
At the end of the skyline,
Where the sun dips into the horizon,
A sulky young Choctaw
Flips the pages of a primer
In the flickers of a street light.
He cannot find what he is looking for.

Apushimataha and Mashulatubi, you are not here!

3.
Two heavyset drunks
Wobble along the road,
Their hapless faces
Flash against the headlight
Of a tribal police car.
As I drive past,
One of them cries out:

O Great Spirit, help us die!

4.
In the Neshoba County Fair Grounds,
Under a century-old tree,
Between two huge political posters,
The sly lips of Bernadine Hickman,
Choctaw Indian Princess,
Sing "God Bless America."

Hugh Fox
E. Lansing, MI

Direction

It's a quiet
non-apocalyptical
Sunday afternoon
heavy with the death of
Summer and Mom calls,
"Aren't the girls there?"
"No, they're still in Kansas City. . ."
"The pictures you sent, Margaret's
a young lady, and Alexandra,
I talked to her on the
phone two weeks ago, such a
mature, deep voice, she ought to
take voice lessons. . .,"
her voice a canoe on
a Renoir-outing-river,
pointellesque in the deep
purples and oranges. . .then
Schizoid-Cubist again,
"If you didn't spend so much
time in those communist
countries!"
"Brazil is a right wing dictator-
ship!"
"Don't call me stupid!"
The mosaic stained-glass day
blurs back and forth between
strut and suicide.

Sheila Nickerson
Juneau, AK

Neighbor

Suppose that old woman—
I have seen her once—
living in that small green house
is related to raspberries.
They alone climb up her walk
every spring and reach till
they can peek in the windows.
I have seen no one—
not even dog or pigeon—
go up that path
in any season. And suppose
that she dies in winter
and that is why her path
is never cleared of snow
and that she rises in spring
with red sap, a vision,
to be met at the door
by her cousins coming for summer.
They carry small bags packed tight,
they gossip like mad.
Leaning against each other,
they dress up,
they whisper of red,
they dream of sleep that follows fruit.
And suppose that we
opened her door in winter
and saw her there,
a tiny nest of roots.

Sarah Denz
Andover, NH

Voters' Choice: Four Cases

Our city hospital is a dark red-brick and concrete sheath artfully lowered over stainless steel and white L-halls: L upon L upon L. Its construction was prideful, hopeful to all, and a mercy at last to put to rest any need for long distance, long-funded ambulance service. Outside the L's bend, stacks of steam rise in gasps from the struggles within, and dissipate over snowy streets. The third L is the busiest L. It might be said that this L seethes, not always with life, but with the instruments and instrumental people vital to disease control — and the aftermath of disease control's failures. Rooms off this L like square boxes. Windows at the far side of each room, also square, like frames to dark tunnels that shoot into the night over the broken brick bones and wood skeletons still standing. These tunnels, it seems, project forever and ever until snow makes white splashes on the polished plate glass. All along the L then is heard that sound like wet Kleenix slapped down. All are reminded of the finiteness of dark tunnels, and other things. Inside the juncture of the L's short arm and long leg is a long, shoulder-high, counter-top desk, also in the form of an L. Behind it, nurses are pale moving mannequins performing dubious tasks at the words of the Ken-doll doctors, university trained. No matter incongruities between ailment and treatment, between treatment and result, their words are gospel and weighty as they lean inwards against the counter. Between the doctors on one side and the nurses, the other, they manage to hold the tall desk up. Patient care proceeds from it, mostly as a sixteen drawer cabinet on wheels, drawer upon drawer upon drawer of pills, capsules, hypodermic needles, orders, names of drugs, names of illnesses, sometimes patients' names, millegrams, times, and dosages; and beneath the drawers: two cubby holes with rolled up, read, and referenced medical magazines. Buzz and light signals are aerial arteries, patient to station and back. In this corolla, but a little apart, old people, senile people, confused people, the hesitant and the halt, are set up in chairs wheeled out from their rooms. Happily they watch the professionals play. Between two such chairs is one tall potted Jade plant, oversized with bloated leaves, misshapen as a Mongoloid child. From its emerald shadow, one thick stubby hand protrudes, merges with it momentarily, extends again, withdraws, and finally drops as a fish gone too far beyond where green shore meets sand. The fingers drum on a linen knee, skillfully, as though setting type. Or playing piano? Or stitchng seams? No one remembers. Then the fingers mold tenderly, the index and middle ones stretched,the ring finger and little one bent back to the thumb. A ballerina's gesture? Or asking for a cigarette? Briefly one tagged: C A R O L in blue print pinned to her collar, wonders, but rustles by anyway. There'd be no reward for her efforts here. Here, time is precious. We horde it, we store it, at the very end we barter with it. On the L the only mark between day and night is the P.A. announcement: "Visiting hoursmmmfff. . .over.   Thankmmff. . .muchmmff cooperation." Sighs and cries like fledgling wing-beats flutter from beds, collect and hover heavily to stain the sterile air, then are wiped away narcotically. Lastly, the people in the hall are wheeled and pilled to bed. The nurses shrug and begin to chat.

Before, in this town, there were four ambulance runs in the business — a thriving one, and it was your choice, or your kin's to be taken to Hanover, to Boston, to Concord, or Claremont. Those days we all had a say and it was a henyard of opinions. When the government offered to match funds with seven medical colleges, and subsidize a regional health care facility on open available land, we all voted for it: the new, in-town hospital, taken to the idea like those hens to the cock. The town in Salisbury, after all, a borough of salis, Anglo-Saxon for "health".

You can see how it's much better now.

Case One

But now Mary-Margaret will not be still. Rue the day she got that walker. Now she thinks she's Marathon Woman. Here she comes, hanging on with her two fists squeezed tight, purple and white, to the top bar of that hip-height cage thing in front of her. She is not altogether rational, but otherwise is typical in size and shape, with thin, gray tufts and cowlicks of hair, a smokey voice, and draping cheeks. She is a believer in heavy perfume and opaque make-up — always, even just to go to bed. "My ring, my ring," she whines. Some look up, some have pity. Most pretend to be too busy. "My wedding ring. Has anyone seen my wedding ring? I don't know where it's got."

Someone spends the time to ask: "Did you give it to a family member?"

Shock. "Oh, no, de-ah, it was mine. It was given to *me*."

"But did you give it to some one to take care. . ."

Mary-Margaret is alreading moving forward again, on her six spindley legs — four aluminum ones and two of flesh and bone, but otherwise similar in size and shape.

"Mary-Margaret, honey, bed-time."

But my wedding ring. . ." Voice rising hysterically.

The nurses roll their eyes in exasperation. One sighs again and rises to lead Mary-Margaret back to her room. "I'll look for your ring in the morning, Mary."

Piano fingers drum silently.

"Bless you, de-ah, bless you. God bless you." But what would she tell Howard, her husband? She could tell him she put into the floor safe for keeping. Or that someone took it while she was being bathed. In bed, she shortly stirs the top sheet and machine knit spread off onto the floor, and curls into a fetal position. Her johnny hikes up to her knees. Her bones tremble and resemble a featherless, motherless chickadee. She's topped with the sweaty spikes of hair and fuzz; there are goosebumps from shoulder to elbow, elbow to fingers, and knees to ankles and over most of her thighs. For all the world she might as well issue a chick's high-pitched squawk: Maawk. Instead she cries a little girl's sobs and remembers she'd buried her ring with her husband.

Maybe in the morning, someone will give her a five-and-dime play ring, a pacifier.

Case Two

All night from room 307 come derelict screams: "Willie. . .Willie. WILLIAM. Come here and help me. Right now. Please. Willie, please come. RIGHT NOW."

Eventually one nurse looks in on Marian. "Cool it, Marian. C O O L I T." And aside, to no one in particular: "Jesus Christ. Don't grow up to be a nurse."

"Willie, I'm cold. I'm cold. William, come and help me. Please. Don't do that to me. WILLIAM." From Marian's wide, dark, toothless mouth come saliva, yells, and finally snores. Rolls of latent fat settle into the dips of the narrow bed. The room, close and overheated, smells of sweat and burned baked-bread — the death smell.

Next morning, every morning, William is the first visitor on the L. Only now Marian is still sleeping. He moves into her room quietly for one of his size, tall and rangy, in his sixth decade, having worked most of four of them in hard shifts at Salis Press. He still sees Salis's specter everywhere. He sees it in the shadows and in the snow collected on the outside sill. He sees it in Marian's wrack-ed face and ruined being. He sees its silhouette which, when wreck-ed, began this town's deterioration to white collars, banks and offices, and uppity retail businesses. The store-keepers, merchants, secretaries and executives, the attorneys, accountants, and the pharmacists all say it's fine now and smile with grins full of large, square teeth, white as glossy blank magazine pages. The druggists, especially, are young and fresh and think it's great fun to quiz a poor senior: "Twist off or child-proof? Tablets or capsules? One a day or two? Medicare card, please. Now your patient I.D. card. The gray one. The gray card. No, gray. GRAY."

Sonny, I am eighty. They are all gray cards to me.

Me, I no longer see her: Salis Press. Once she was king-pin here, printer of all the region's weeklies and monthlies. Over a hundred employees and best pay in the state — some of which went to good, to church, some to drink, some to drug, which, I guess, led to this: Polytheism, worship of many white polyester gods and their angels in winged caps. Maybe my views are blocked now, by pressboard walls, these rubbery leaves, and cataracts, but I can tell William's face in there (although he'd not know me). His thin blue eyes narrow as the L's lights flicker on at a quarter to eight. For as long as it takes to raise twenty switches to bright, the spreading yellow mouth moves through the L swallowing any small privacy, any peace, just like the City white-washing the town in neon, that very city south which once was the mama wolf-spider carrying and nurturing the little wolf-spiderling towns on her back, feeding them even after they'd grown, then connecting her little sibling towns with her six fine tendril legs: Routes 114, 193, 212, Routes 23, 4, and 89. Now that same wolf-spider mama's turned to feast on her babies. Where on earth for a spider here, now? A cleaning woman, a pyramid of pink rayon steppes, her uniform strained over the half-dozen bulges between her waist and her neck, slaps the air and stabs through Marian's door, 'round the room, for dust balls and silk filament webs — imaginary ones, because she'd just swabbed through here yesterday, and the day before, and the day before. She jabs a mop under the bed, pokes a feather duster at the mirror, and straightens scattered stray back issues of NuMed Journal. At the rising sounds: tinny trays, collected pills, flushed toilets, and running faucets, William sinks his head low between hard shoulders, then moves to kneel and lay it on his daughter's breast. Vociferous awake, she is oddly ghostly now. He can't hear her rasp or her heart-beat over the clink-a-clink ticking off of amber droplets into a vein. The clink-a clinking will go on long after the patient is gone. May be hours before anyone finds the time to come. Protein and glucose will flow, umimpeded by need, through veins and kidneys and bladder. Yellow stain on disposable sheet. Williwm should really make his mind up to sign those release forms. Marian won't even know what's what.

And she can play such a vital role in the progress of science.

Case Three

By the desk, Mrs. Follansbee waits patiently on a gurney. The lines of her face are a delicate intaglio as the spaces of flesh between them are as white as the sheet. Ceiling lights sear bars through her eyelids, onto her retinas, the good right one and the bad left. She's been ready and prepped in the hall like this for over an hour. An hour and forty-five minutes go by before a husky young man with a bear's beard and much curly hair jumps out the shuttering elevator doors and yips a loud: "Good morning. How are you? Hot? cold?" He wears only half-white — his shirt, as befits his status. From his blue jeans hip pocket, a current copy of NuMed rudely beetles and flops its arrogance. "Your doctors are ready for you," the fellow is casual, and wheels her off, around the corner, out of sight.

The hand from the Jade raises a paper cuplet of wine-red tomato juice: A toast to Follansbee.

Case Four

I'd hardly finished breakfast, not even had a wash, when they wheeled me out to tha hall for another day of waiting and watching. Dried Wheatena itches at the corners of my mouth, and fuzzy beneath my nose is a lick of that watery tomato juice, its cup of cardboard marked with measures crumpled in my hand. God, I wish I had a smoke, just one cigarette. But someone would have to come with me and stay with me in the solarium. Ah, the solarium: the only irregular shape on the ward, with a big bay window where a man can smoke and think and ruminate on the plethora of dog-eared NuMeds with their marginal drolleries and underscored rubrics like medievel psalters. Dare I ask to go? At the desk is all chaos turning into the day's order. At the end of the counter medications are ready. In the linen room, bed changes are assigned. Back again to the top of the desk: By now they've all gone to their busy-ness and would not understand an old man's need. These young people have no bad habits. They call us: High Blood Pressure, Angina, Diabetes, Cancer lung, Cancer tongue, Cancer rectal. Even when I made my phone call, *I'd* at least had the courtesy to address *them* right and proper: "Rescue Squad, *sirs,*" but myself as simply: "Heart Trouble". They found me. I did try: "My name's Roberts." I anguished it out.

"Rob? Bob? What?"

"Well, it's Bobby actually." I badly needed to be familiar with some of all this efficiency, but I don't think they heard — the radio and sirens considered; and I've no idea what they could see through the cast display of red and yellow flashers. It's our city ambulance, an award winner. It can reach our city hospital from any location in the county in six-point-five minutes or less. Chances are nill you'll die on the way. But on the way you'll be carefully checked. You'll be peeled and prodded for color like corn on the cob, or stuck like a melon to see if you're ripe.

We voted.

Some people want to vote over again. But I say: "Oh, no, you don't want to do that. Look what voting got us the last time." It was the last time. If there are children tomorrow, they'll read in history books about my decades and the ones just before: The Decades of Voting. Now choice is an ancient archaic species. It's shed its skin and metamorphosed. Impossible to recognize.

But if I had it to do over, I'd do nothing different. I *was* good.

I *can* set type— Rumford's best. William passed me by on his way to Upper Management; I stayed at my key board, my big console to lives, in charge of idea from first draft to proof, could set more type than a dozen hand compositors. A journal like NuMed, circulation: three thousand, took a three-thousand pound roll — good, heavy, quality paper for NuMed — for each of pages one through tow hundred or more, all to be spread to class rooms, waiting rooms, doctors' rooms, bed-rooms, official rooms, and hospital solariums. Medical students poured into the town, to this gleaming new unit here, like moths to the flame they came, from Boston, from Washington, from New York and further. Each clutched a studied NuMed to his chest, pausing to mark it with colored felt-tips, prizing it. Compared to it, all other luggage was so much excess baggage. And I — I set the matrices to all these lives. (If you know what color felt-tip your personal M.D. uses, and where he keeps his NuMeds, you can save yourself a consultation cost, because whatever he's read is what he'll do to you, or tell you not to do.)

I wish I had a cigarette.

When NuMed's prestige and clientele grew, we took on more pressmen; the best of us took an apprentice. Things looked good, and William said, "We'll get you your own full-time assistant." "Nothing doing," I said, "I can handle it." I couldn't. Blame's not entirely mine. The steady gains of NuMed's circulation cut off the life-flow at Salis (which had long since cut off business with the local smaller potatoes). When the esteemed journal's contract expired, its owners signed on with another firm, a larger, more modern, quicker (quicker that I?) press in that city south. Salis Press closed and filed for bankruptcy. "That's okay," people said, "we need the space for the hospital grounds now." William shook his head. We all applied for unemployment.

I *can't* play the piano, although sometimes I tap keys on my knees. Frowned upon here. Arm gestures are too strenuous, they say. Not allowed. No matter. The clink-a-clinking of that timed

I.V. is similar sound to the sliding of slugs into galley. That's my music and I'm glad to hear it. Enjoy it more with a cigarette. But everyone is busy. Time costs. All the rooms are filled now, except for Mrs. Follansbee's down at the hall's very end. Wonder who they'll fill her room with. Because, of course, she won't be back. It's her right eye they'll cut for someone who can better use it and use it longer. Everywhere on Floor 2 —Pediatrics, anxious parents and children elderly in their awareness, stare at the ceiling, that is, the floor of Geriatrics. Wonder who'll go down in that end room. I overheard. . . (I'd been in the bathroom. I can still do that myself, although they stand there anyway, at the lockless door, waiting for that cord to wail when it's yanked by some fallen or stuck toilet sitter.) I overheard two nurses say Mary-Margaret might be next. Although there's others worse, I can't help but wonder when my turn will be.

Still. Glad to be where I am. Glad to have fallen sick in time to fall under the Salis policy's grandfather clause. Otherwise, I'd have been put right away into that room on the end. Glad to not see out today, to miss the factory's final interment, to not see people stricken daily out there among the vestiges: the severed eight-room Federalist homes, the plot allotments of the park land, the hollow book shops and the movie house with all the air sucked out of it, the lemon ice stand, the bandstand, the baseball field's grandstand, behind which boys like William became half-grown men, and half-grown men like me became men, teasing the girls, playing with them and setting them in the sun to mature. Even on gray days, shadows shed by sycamores and cedars, not to mention the Press's pitched roof, were hardly gloomy. They were Fortune's wings blessing. The front gate to Salis Press was ugly grate, black rod-iron, Heaven's gate. Through it came all our Dads, five nights a week, the tenth being Pay Day. My eyes on mine: on Pay Day he had a check in his pocket and a smile on his face. All the fathers wore the same, and treated as many as fell within the arch of their arms, to bubble-gum and beer at Cheney's Mercantile.

Now we're told: Stay out of the sun. Ruined Follansbee's eyes. Wrinkled Marian's skin fast as a drought shrivels no-man's orchard. I'm not sure I understand things now that we've become a city. Feudal soft-ware and green screens decide rooting and seeding and hy-breeding of fruits now. I'm better off in here. I would, however, like a smoke.

William is leaving, shuffling along like twice his age. He'd not know me; can't face reality.

Be like my friend here, William, the potted Jade, independent, self-sufficient, needing only a drop of water here and again, strong, sturdy, forever *alive*.

Whatever you do, don't go out in that sun. It will spot your skin and make you old.

Linda Hutton
Coeur d'Alene, ID

Dawn's Arrival

The night wears a crown of stars
Set off by a shawl of clouds as
She draws her velvet sleeve across the moon
And nods to the approaching sun.
Before retiring, she slips off her rings
To hang them on the pines
Where they wink like fireflies,
Distracting us from her departure.

Ralph J. Fletcher, Jr.
Bronx, NY

A Great Man

One night on a camping trip
a man whose named face I can't recall
took me a few steps from the fire
and told me in a serious voice
that I could be a great man,
how greatness was within my grasp.

I was ten years old,
old enough to squeeze those words
and thrill with them in the firelight.
I envisioned greatness as swelling force:
stunning, broad, inevitable.

I remembered those words growing up
through church tedium, odd school hours,
summer afternoons watching baseball on tv
when I should have been playing outside;
I recalled and knew the elation you get
thrust from a lush and forgotten dream.

Today I can do no more than marvel
at how the crafty years can sculpt
a boy's vague, fertile features
into a face so specific and narrow.

Perverse or sincere, those spoken words
started me on a great inward journey.
What had that man possibly seen
to plant such a dread and barbed seed,
a glowing, half-taunted irritation
coated with layer upon insulating layer,
to grow into the secret, misshapen pearl
                in an otherwise ordinary life?

R. Parks Lanier, Jr.
Radford, VA

Vertical Hold

I watch as wasps
attack the window
force field glass
channeling horizontal
intentions into
vertical aggravations.
I watch a woman
watching me cup wasps
in my bare hands
there in the restaurant.
Reflected in the glass,
she surprises her blouse
with gravy because I
never flinch, because I
only stare at hands
that channel horizontal
intentions into vertical
despair. She does not know
wasps with yellow faces
never sting.

Paul Weinman
Albany, NY

Back By The Raspberries

Back by the raspberries, he stands
and stares where a path had led
to spring peepers. Out by the pond
choked thick with alga and leaves
rotting brown. When his feet were smaller,
he had followed his father's steps
so quiet through the moss and throbs
of amphibian nightness.
Tried to imitate his easy stride
and twists through brambles grown long
in flowers all white.
But he'd always get scratched at least once
in that thinnish manner of raspberry thorn.
Skin would part so clean -
leave a line slow to be traced by blood.
They'd sit at hickory roots along the shore.
Watch some ducks and talk over each day.
Share what both saw first . . . a stare,
splash of small fish taking a moth below;
a ripple of turtle about to surface . . .
what mom had been like.
Father'd been buried back by the raspberries.
Next to her where the path
made that smooth bend,
then, straightened again.

Noel M. Valis
Athens, GA

Being Good

There is this urge to be
useful like polish or cleaner.
Indispensable to those you love.
To grow handles and spigots
and be poured endlessly on the ground.
Find yourself babbling the right words,
emptying the cookie jar of the alphabet
to discover, later, the mold you used
is minus certain valuable letters
you won't read anymore.
Remaking the bed forever
while the impress you smooth out
is human elsewhere.
While you lie in it, hoping to catch
a fugitive warmth,
the thrust of being.
Those natural impulses
you can't strangle deep enough.

L. Snydal
San Jose, CA

Cut Finger

Right to the bone, I sliced into the tip
Of my left index finger. I could feel
The flap of flesh, the blade, the blood, the heel
Of French bread on the board. I heard the drip
Of snow slow off the eaves. A two-hour trip
To town and stitches made no sense. To seal
This seam before the juices could congeal,
Restore the finger, ravel up the rip,
We wound, my wife and I, strip after strip
Of gauze and tape and gauze. And now it's real
And whole except it's learned how to conceal
Its heats and hurts. And now I have a chip
Of frozen flesh to carry on my hand,
A bit of death to own and understand.

Don Thornton
New Iberia, LA

Jeannie

Jeannie will risk
dissecting your heart
for jizsaw puzzle pictures
to use as heart breakers
for fabricating melodic lyrics
to be sung at home wreckings
while winds bend marsh grass
to touch the sandy beach
where she lay and loved
the sounds of gulls
and the roar of swells
pounding the rhythm
of her hushed passion.

She held men;
crazed, wild-eyed,
burying their sorrows
in the nests
of her sparrow breasts.

She was psychoanalyzed
on a Galveston beach
as she and the analyst
built sandcastles
for Dali landscapes.

Linda Ulmer
Port Hueneme, CA

Summer's End

Somebody stole the summer.
Someone uprooted the orange geraniums
from within their red adobe pots and winged
the warmth from the breath of the summer breeze.
Someone sucked the juice out of the strawberries
and left them wrinkled like raisins,
black and dying in the sun.

Somebody stole the summer.
Someone erased the song from the Paper Bubble shell.
Emptiness crushed its skeleton into
coral powder which bled into the sand.
Someone sponged the silver shimmer from the ocean waves;
then vacuumed up the sunbeams, threw away the bag,
and left me standing in this purple haze
without a map to guide my way.

Somebody stole the summer.
Surely the culprit's footprints
must have etched the yellow sand;
but in the lonely distance stilted Pippets
echo. . .no
just one word lies pressed in sandskrit.
Its black stamp stains the milk white shore.
Just one word reflects from sand to sky -
Good-bye.

Somebody stole the summer

William Scott Conlogue
Atlanta, GA

Luther

Across the lawn
Or field I should say.
Luther starts for the beaten path-
Between - a fence no longer there.
With pail in hand
He meets me at the door,
A conversation sure to ensue -
Of the weather,
Or politics maybe too;
Until ambling along his way
To his place of rest.
Days of summer Luther could be seen
With mower before him
An acre, it seemed, left in his wake.
A man of many years,
Chopping wood -
His youth to retain;
A bike he would ride to town
Or wherever he hap to go.
In amzement of myself -
Luther, I'm afraid, is no longer here
except in dear held memories.

G.O. Clark
Davis, CA

Nostalgia

As I watch the
bicyclists pass by,
one momentarily stands
out from all the rest,

bent over his
ten speed handlebars—
chin, nose, eyes
piercing the autumn air—

looking just like the
flesh and blood reincarnation
of a 50's Pontiac hood ornament,
that chrome and plastic

Indian chief, who mutely rode
those uneasy, cold war
highways; symbol of strength
and broken promises.

Frank Finale
Pine Beach, NJ

Gnome

That gnome of an apple tree
where green boys
dropping from its crooked branches
whooped, "GERONIMO!"
is still there. A vacant lot once
laced with lightning
bugs, asterisks of blue chicory,
chirruping crickets
and a throb of frogs, now grows
twelve-story apartments
that blink in the dark. Between the first
story and second,
the gnome breathes in the traffic.
Every year,
blooming from its dark niche, it dazzles
its space white
snowing over the bottle caps,
styrofoam cups
and piecemeal litter of lives. Still
bears fruit.

Babatunde Solarin
Euliss, TX

The Storyteller

Once upon a time,
Before the gods
Took away the Chicken's will to fly;
There lived a people
In the valley
Where the spring's water
Is sweeter than Sugar-cane's.
They were your father's father;
They were your mother's mother.

I am the storyteller,
As black as the hands
That gave me life.
Look upon my chest,
Behold century-old breasts
In their virgin dance,
Hear the war drum
That have laid silent for ages,
The scream
Caught in the throat
Of slain warriors
And feel the horror
In their eyes.
Taste the aroma of yam porridge
From the fire
Melting the morning mist.

I am the storyteller
I have been here before your time.

Kevin J. Lavey
Washington, DC

Seafarer

A young man steps through the hatch and out onto the deck of the ship. So strange and unnatural are his movements that it's as though we see him through the secondary means of a jerky black and white home movie. Why peace or tranquility or inclusion or love or even a small part of one of those has passed him by to settle within the heart of the next man is undiscoverable. He ranges across the deck so drunk he can hardly guide himself unitl he gets to the railing where he holds on and looks out at the disturbed ocean. The water has been churning for days. The mate told him that there was a hurricane off the Florida coast and that they were decreasing their speed until they could see what direction it would take. On his bunk, beneath his pillow, lies a note which he promises himself will be his last words to the world.

I am going over, he thinks.

"Say, Jack," he hears behind him and he turns, but no one is there. Instead it is the voice of his good friend, Jim Barks, with whom in his first year at college he shared a dormitory room. The singular voice has acted like a serum which conjures memories from their sepulchre in his brain. They rise to form.

He and Jim stop beneath the trees on campus at the University of Michigan. They are both holding books and they are the young avatars of college men, both the representatives of something so much larger than themselves that neither could begin to comprehend it.

"How'd the exam go?" Jim asks.

"All right," says Jack. "It's over."

"You're keeping that 4.0 intact, eh? We're counting on you. Without you the world crumbles and splits apart and then the plague begins and. . ."

"You've been hanging out with Sorenson, right? Young Yeats?"

Jim Barks and Jack are both graced with good looks and their body language suggests supreme confidence. Their friendship will extend beyond the campus grounds and college talk, each's voice clear to the other through letters, though neither could possibly know that one week after graduating ceremonies they would never see one another again. People grow apart is all that can be said.

"Jack." He hears now his father's voice. His life has slipped away from the charmed luxury of young malehood and the uncensored approval of seemingly everyone he meets. He and his father have wrestled and punched each other. A lamp has been hurled against the wall; he has smashed his foot through an irreplaceable stained-glass window pane in the dining room door. When the momentum for such destruction first began he cannot say. He always remembers this time as though it were something he'd heard about, something he finds hard to believe of people. He's been at home from college a year and he and his mother and father sit at the kitchen table with their hands folded in front of them, with, as they've told him, most every option available to them gone, talking of final things.

"Jack, your mother and I have shown a great deal of patience. We don't know what else to do."

Yes they had, he thinks, shown a great deal of patience. They had. For months he has been coming home at night as drunk and as drugged as a human can possibly get without stopping the heart and expiring altogether. They have asked him many times why he has felt the need to do it and even now while he sits with them he cannot answer that question, though he would like to. Both of his parents are haggard and exhausted and he is able to recognize in their faces that the worry he's caused them has etched itself permanently into the cast of their expressions.

"Son, what would you think of a place that can offer you things your mother and I don't seem able to. We're. ." His father can't finish. His mother is crying, holding her face in her hands like a chalice.

The scene reels on and he stands up from the table burdened

with himself. . .yet not contrite. He has asked no one or nothing for forgiveness and in a way he is glad that something is finally going to happen. Exhaustion has brutalized him and he has been left slugging wildly at the world, he cannot plant himself solidly in place to once more begin and now it has come to this, a refuge for his retreat at the instruction of his parents. That's all right, he thinks, I will survive. Because of his father's job he has lived in Tokyo, Cairo, London, Pittsburgh, Sacramento, Tallahassee, Austin, Seattle, Milwaukee, Kansas City, and Detroit, and so deep down somewhere he knows there is a fibre of himself that is indestructable. In his adult life it has not been available, but it will be, it has to.

"Fine," he says, "I'm ready."

"Jack." Again he swings around to look behind himself, hoping to see a familiar face accompanying that familiar voice. Instead, the deck is empty. Metal creaks under the stress of the ocean. Shadows lie like iron against the bulkheads.

"Jack." It is his wife. How he could have possibly married a woman—the unthinkable ability of man procuring for himself a formula for reprieve, the calculations of which are so improbable as to be figured in another universe and beamed directly to him bypassing all human sense—is something that could not be imagined outside the borders of a cartoon strip. He remembers himself talking to her of children, of a job, of a good life and this talk had the exquisite exterior of something permanent and fine and properly theirs. They move into a trailer park home and she becomes pregnant and he feels himself rooting to the spot. He sees the child grow until six months old then, without premeditation, while out on a walk one night, goes to the Greyhound bus station and buys a ticket to Memphis, Tennessee and disappears from her life.

"Jack." But she is gone. He hitchhikes continuously and he is lulled into a peacefulness that comes from the steady travel, from the discovery that the absence of responsibility in his life has in itself an eminence granted him by people he meets in bars and gas stations. Thus he lives, inviolable in his estrangement, until one afternoon in Little Rock, Arkansas he is shot in the arm during a robbery attempt in a 7-Eleven while standing in line waiting to buy an orange slurppee. He talks to the doctor about his life, the man reminds him of his grandfather, and somehow out of that conversation Jack emerges with a job on a merchant marine vessel.

He is twenty-eight years old and he has been on the ship six months and there is no moon tonight. The stars, he thinks, are an act of God so intricately beautiful that he can't imagine why man was left incomplete. The ocean rolls and heaves as though huge animals lumber just beneath the surface. He loves intimately what he sees before him; he loves the profound fact of his body, the two legs, the trunk, the arms, the hands, the neck, the head; he loves the vastness of his thoughts. A seagull nailed to the sky flies just off the fantail and he looks to it for steady reassurance for a moment before clumsily arching his leg up to the top cable of the railing. He hesitates when he hears his name being called from somewhere, from somewhere he hopes he's been called all along, the hope of which he's been too distracted to consider.

Marc Widershien
Brookline, MA

1984 Desideratum

in the sullen acts
and arts
the romantic consciousness
fades to a crystal
in which we were told
was the consciousness of a race

the blind murder
orders the impulse

in the numbing tale
which only serves to entertain
we forget that nothing changes
the watercourse of history
played out all too carefully
in a patented script

you broke that flow,
Eric Blair
without the derangement of one sense
you gave us the program
the scenario
the finish

like an inscrutable toy
we play with a date
which for you was a reversal of 1948
a curtain drawn over the shell of water
religion orphaned on an unscaleable mountain
you brought us back out of the void
into the collective darkness—
and what remains in the shell?
a blinding light which escapes
whenever we break bread

Emma Crobaugh
Highland Beach, FL

Burning New Questions

The World holds diagrams
of sugar cane and banana groves
flowing green
down slopes to the sea.

New craters opened in my ears yesterday,
leaving me blackened, desolate.
Bubbling lava
streams in my blood, burning new questions.
My bones lay deep in volcanic ash,
sulphur makes my breathing difficult.

I gesture resignation —

perfume of wildflowers
erupts in morning breath —
a bubbling spring
streams into my blood with sweet water.

Linda R. Bell
Knoxville, TN

Before The Days Of Divorce

He thought himself a failure.
She had convinced him.
You could see it in his face.
By other people's standards, perhaps he was.

How his eyes sparkled
when one of us kids came in.
He'd greet the boys by butting heads.
I was the only girl.
We'd go for the billy-goat greeting
only when his wife wasn't watching.
(She was one of the other people.)

I remember how he'd always buy me a Brownie cola
when we went riding in his rundown pickup.
(She drove the brand new Buick.)

Long after he sold his chestnut mare
the barometer in his bones
was still predicting weather.
(She never did believe him.)

This hardy outdoorsman loved sassafras tea
almost as much as pepper on ice cream.
(I always thought that was just to annoy her.)

For eighty winters he bowed against the world
(and to her every whim),
but for two last years he fanned the fire,
fought her with flaming words,
as if he knew the end was near.
And when it finally came . . . he was glad.

Bernard Forer
Sarasota, FL

Manic-Depressive Syndrome

Her life is a lake
Whose tiny waves intrude continually upon the shore
Where wet sands glitter like flecks of glass
In the rays of the feverish sun.
Her words are like endless stands of trees
That push the grass to the waters.
They are tall and repetitive,
Fed by inner springs of emotion,
Like prisoners paroled and set free,
Startled by the sunlight.
Her phrases conjure back her youthful years in minute detail
And beat upon the listener
Without remorse.
She is garrulous and tireless, consumed in surface gaiety.

But then winter comes.
The lake freezes,
And the waves have retreated to hibernation.
Trees stand bare, shivering in the wind.
The geyser of words has retreated into the earth.
She herself has become immobile, frozen,
Incapable of function.
She floats on lithium clouds into an aching oblivion,
Waiting for the ice to crack.

Here is her tragedy:
No glorious spring to waken slowly the rebirth of life,
And no sparkling autumn
To presage the coming of softly falling snow.

She lives in a world of two seasons.

Jon Kyle Murray
Norman, OK

The Crazy Crane

Have you ever noticed how the crane
    stands on one leg alone?
Is it an act of balancing -
    Does it ever make him groan?

That crazy crane stands there alone
    as if he didn't know
Just which leg to choose to use
    if the wind would chance to blow

Just watching him standing there
    almost makes me feel the need,
to call to him, "Your stance is great"
    but I s'pose he wouldn't heed.

Kiva
Elk, CA

Bear Creek

My sister and I walked
the two miles
down the railroad tracks,
chasing lizards
in and out of the ties.
The cattle grazed on the hills
slow and lazy.
We swam down into that
ice water snow water.
Swam against the rapids.
The excitement of getting
to the top.
So much work,
going to the bottom,
then surfacing,
the whole world a single light,
shimmering through the alders.
"Swim out to the sandbar,
you can make it."
We went down for the third time
then came up to see
three or four big guys,
friends of hers
diving in.
We were children of the sun,
the afternoons
blackened our skin.
Pulled to the earth
we set our rhythms there,
breathing and resting,
the same as the wind
that came up strong

around 4 o'clock.
There was time then
to watch the water spiders
skipping across the stilled creek
and to listen to the far off train whistle,
which would then
come barreling over the trestle,
a signal of the late hour,
the long, hot and dusty walk home.

First appeared in the **Mendocino Review.**

— ★ —

Paul Weinman
Albany, NY

Speaking Easily

We were invited to a picnic
under thepines with seventeen deaf mutes
and a phongraph that didn;t work.
Oh yes, there also was a girl - young
six who had her wrist in a cedar chest
crying while stories were burning
to be told through thumbs and various
waves of hand. I wait wide
then scream while they laugh
and she surrounds my tummy
with talkative hands.

Linda Nemec Foster
Big Rapids, MI

Aunt From West Virginia

For sixteen years she thought the sky was lost
in orange, not in blue. The steel mills owned
her life completely, blindly, even down
to colors. How the laundry smouldered rust
on lines, on shelves, on faceless men she pursed
her lips for. Empty days when light and sun
got clogged in valleys, turned out bad and wrong.
Like sisters, pregnant, skins becoming coarse.

The last years now belong to husband; someone boring, clean, from Midwest plains. Her hair
just slightly gray, she fills her house with prisms.
So many colors she can hold in her
pale hand. Unlike the stillborn infants, mum
and blue. Unlike the air: uncolored, clear.

Kelly Averill
Sylvania, OH

Mr. Poe

Your ghost, Mr. Poe,
Reads over my shoulder
And your breath on my neck, with the storm outside
Has left a chill in my bone-house.
The candle flame dances, your mad orbs watch me
From the cover of my paperback text.

You were here with me for dinner, Mr. Poe.
The raw venison roast looked sinister, somehow,
Lying on the drainboard, severed flesh and bone.
The blood ran over the porcelain edge,
Dripped into the sink and stained the water
Where beheaded scallion bulbs floated,
Root hair flying wild and pale.

I chopped cloves of garlic for the roast, thinking,
"Thus I bind thy powers, Mr. Poe!"

But your ghost remains.
My blackberry tea is dark like wine, and hot.
I set the cup by the tarantula's glass box
And the weaver-goer lifted a furry foreleg,
Contemplating the swaying steam ghost condensed on the glass.

I believe that your evil tarns and dripping corpses
Will follow me to my dreams and haunt me there;
And so here I sit, early into the morning,
Knowing your ghost awaits in my bed.

Beth C. Warrell
Williamstown, VT

In Whispers

This is a poem about murder

Family heirlooms, photos, scrapbooks,
come to me as the last natural
successor who might read
clippings, puzzle
over dim sepia strangers.
There is also a small trunk
with handsown, unworn garments,
its secrets as tight as seams.

It is 1887 in a small town.
There is shame in the meadow,
seeping in the orchard; an image
locked in the trousseau trunk
to fade with daguerreotype faces.

There are things women do not talk about.
Terrible things always with us.
Headlines scream them; officials proclaim
they cannot happen here. Mothers
pass the fear to daughters.

John L. D. Backman
Salem, MA

The Muted Palette, Burning

We fill the photograph, wrapped around each other.
On my lapel, a grinning carnation,
symbol of weddings. I look into the camera,
but you refuse - instead, you adore me,
an innocence shadowing your eyes. Our greens and pinks
are rosebuds with futures.

We are more gaunt now. The year at hand has focused
on different subjects in the scene. At first
I shone, growing, all the time, more handsome, using
photograph as mirror: checking the old carnation's
innocence against my new self, growing taller.

In time your frame grew more interesting. You are
no longer pink. Your eyes carry
an oblivious wisdom. Your gaze is intact,
though less clear: our colors have muddied.
We love the clashes, but their causes are veiled:
what kind of film changes our hues?

This muted palette forces me
to look for clues. I gaze at the space around us -
the head of a man behind me. He is a stranger
to me; his nose emerges from my shoulder. Why
is he standing there, his bald pate captured
for all time?

No one knows his original reason.
He is the background to our colors,
a curious delineation of the bond between us:
immortalized, yet unknown.

Virginia West
Holt, MI

Winding Trail To Home

Green meadows are gone from the
                                    valley
And perfume of the rose brings
                                    tears,
As I travel back in memories
Thru long lonely years.
Days of youth have faded
My steps have slower grown,
As I view the browning meadow
Down the winding trail of home.
Gone are the sweet days of yesterday
Loved ones left for their heavenly
                                    home
Still I cling to the golden memories
As I walk the trail to home.
Carefree years flash before me
As a child once again I see,
The meadow so green in the Springtime
Where I dreamed 'neath the spreading
                                    tree.
Like a story each chapter must end
As each page today I review
To find sunshine and sorrow
In this passing world I knew.

William H. Hansell
Sheboygan, WI

On A Hill

we strain in opposite directions
a dark girl on a bike going up
me in the grass near the wood

her hips roll smoothly
a motion like treading water
or running in a dream

my body lurches forward
strains to keep the pace
jolted from my usual stride

her soprano greeting
a shiver over my skin

Sally Love Saunders
Malvern, PA

Word Pictures

Framed in the city window
an all black cat poised in prayer position.
The short punk rock hair
on the passing long-legged teenager
must have been caught
in a pencil sharpener,
the wood shavings from the pencil
still sticking.
Tourists wearing
carefully selected clothes
augmenting their hometown styles,
while those whose homes are the streets
seem more relaxed.
The wind whipping it all
as though an electric mixer
trying to make a bowl of mashed potatoes.
High rise apartments houses;
human honey combs.

Marc Widershien
Brookline, MA

Martha Graham At 90

Tragedy is the razor's edge we walk
even when the head tests the pillow
in the dense hours when dreams
make their delicate demands
to send us searching for the missing
ticket stub

a gesture placed in balance
like the undertaker's sleight of hand

Her jawstrings open to antiquity
the motions centered in the essence
of motion

beauty like an awakened dawn
tense like a butterfly

counterweight
the poem in its various phases
obligated to the words

there is a lesson
in an old master's eye
a journey and a burning

the body spherical like our turning earth

Joseph Awad
Richmond, VA

Hospitals

They no longer eavesdrop on your chest,
Peer down your throat,
Put pincer fingers to your pulse
Or ask you where it hurts.

Your corpus is hooked up to a machine
That prints out data on a screen.

Technicians in the basement lab
Argue over shadows in your X-rays.
Others, at microscopes, squint into hells
Lifted from sputum, urine samples, blood,
Where hideous creatures writhe and reproduce
And slaughter their own kind.

You have no strength to watch the television.
It magnifies to human scale
The micrococci of the blood's infections—
Hatred, greed, adulteries, murders, wars,
Rumors of war.
This sick room traffic is a final outrage.
They swarm to check, not you, but tube and gauge.

My unexpected visit and the press,
Momentary, of my hand on yours,
Lifts your drooping lids. You ramble:
"Remember that first day we drove to Richmond?
The old Chevvy. . .open windows. . .
Springtime air gushing. . .
That pastoral scene we passed along the road;
Green slopes and the graceful necks of horses

Nibbling grass. . .
The white-washed barn above them. . .and beyond,
A steeper, greener rise. . .a house. . .
White clapboard and rose trellises,
Leafy oaks towering. . .higher still,
The white clouds. . .free. . .and that delicious blue. . .

The nurses interrupt, your breath half gone;
Time to turn the respirator on.

Adam Szyper
Kendall Park, NJ

Do Not Complain To Distant Friends

I had written once to a distant friend
About my suffering HERE and he replied:
"You have no idea how I suffer HERE."

Thus I had told him about spots on the moon
And canals on the planet Mars and he to me about
Black Holes in space and the disappearance of dinosaurs.

Our eyes are immersed in slushy puddles
And everyone in his own puddle
Sees only his own monster

Ken Stone
Portlandville, NY

Name

[to Katherine]

Why was she special
this woman whom I loved?
Was it the soft grey of her eyes
or the bell-sound of her laugh?
I still smell the glow of her perfume,
the aroma of the female in love.
But by whose accusations
did I sever our belonging;
or was it my own jealousy,
that ultimate irresponsibility,
which did the deed? When
at sunset's fall we kissed
that final time rather than put
our goodbye into words, why
did my tears cease as soon as
you were out of sight? What
accident of imperfection caused
me not to call you back
but allowed me only to put my
emotions into this poem?

Diana Azar
Irvine, CA

A Matter Of Principle

One morning as my housemate and I were about to watch an important television rerun, I noticed a man coming up the rural hillside road toward our modest rented house. Something dangled from his hand. The front window, no cleaner than you would expect the windows to be where two bachelors lived, prevented me from making out just what it was.

"Who's that?" Douglas uncurled his long legs, setting his huge slippered feet flat down on the floor with that same stamp of conviction that marked his beliefs.

I peered through the double obstacle of smudgy glasses and the cloudy window at the stranger coming up the dusty road. "I was about to ask you the same question," I said. "He doesn't look much like a salesman."

"No," Douglas agreed. "He doesn't."

Inevitably, the knock came. Douglas arched the bushy brows shading his creek-green eyes. A few unruly hairs rushed the bridge of his nose like weeds erupting through cracks in a city sidewalk. No matter how often he trimmed them—for he disliked disorder even more than violence—new ones appeared, more perverse still, lending to otherwise well-behaved features a tangle of surprise. "Not shy, is he?" he said, for the raps had been insistent, loud. Since I had seen the match in town the night before and Douglas hadn't, I rose to answer the door.

Before me stood a sun-dried, middle-aged, balding farmer, the color and shape of an oven-roasted peanut. He wore the denim overalls and cowboy boots common to these bare hills which roll around the Columbia River Basin like undulating fences of smooth stone. Thick, work-worn fingers coiled round the black throat of what turned out to be a rooster. The rooster, evident even to my shortsighted eyes, was dead.

"You the owner a this house?"

"No," I said, "but I live here."

"You own them chickens and that big red bird out back?"

"Just a minute. I'll get you the guy who does."

I stepped aside to let Douglas look down on the bowlegged farmer from twelve inches of superior height. The tartan robe he wore recalled his skirted ancestors, drifting, in clouds of mist and fog, down from their highland villages to break in bloody thunderclaps over the Roman settlements below. Accompanied by the eerie whine of mournful bagpipes, Scots slow-danced into battle, striking tones of such deep terror into Roman soldiers' hearts that only rude Germanic legions—barbarians like the Scots themselves—proved effective against them.

None of this fierce history could now be seen in Douglas, unless it was the way he jerked the ends of his plaid belt together, as if not merely to secure his robe but to garrot his waist. "What can I do for you?" he asked. His lush moustache, a perfect rainbow streaked with red and rusty gold, engulfed his upper lip so that, when Douglas spoke, the words came forth as if from an oracular dark hole. There were many, in and out of our office in town, who set great store by anything that Douglas said, but the farmer clearly was not one of them. A jacks-size ball rotated slowly in his dry hard cheek. No doubt he'd never heard of the wall Hadrian built to keep Douglas' ancestors up in the hills where they belonged, for, turning his head to one side, the farmer spat a dark irreverent stream of chewed tobacco to the ground, curdling the dust where it fell.

"You got somethin' out back musta got out last night." The farmer raised the hand that held the dead rooster aloft. "Looky here what it done to my Lucky."

Douglas and I looked.

"You sure it was mine?" Douglas' tone was almost free of any hint of challenge that might transform encounter into confrontation.

"It's yours all right."

The farmer thrust the dead bundle of feathers forward. Instinctively, Douglas recoiled. For whatever his ancestry, he was like me a city dweller, as unused to the sight and smell of death as to the blood-soaked spectacle of birth. He had taken the hillside house to show, by his example, that rural life need not mean callous exploitation of the land and animals upon which it depended. The house for Douglas was a grand experiment to test his principles, for he believed that principles, unless applied, are empty pretenses, and empty pretenses are graver threats to civilized society than no principles at all. In the city planning office where we worked, Douglas often reminded his followers that the coarse inhabitants of the river basin must be gently drawn into the widening circle of light the city sought to spread over the countryside.

My own motives for taking the house were less lofty.

Before joining the ranks of Douglas' disciples, I wanted to see whether, in his private life, Douglas applied his principles as scrupulously as he did at work.

"See here?" the farmer said. The fingers of his free hand disappeared into the ebony plush that had once been Lucky. Deep gashes gaped out from the gray flesh underneath. "And lookie here. . .see that?" Unceremoniously twisting Lucky's neck, the farmer's thick fingers parted the down to reveal a rake of slashes, the sluices through which Lucky's life's blood had run out.

Douglas and I stared.

"Jesus," Douglas breathed, stirring the reddish gold forest that brushed his upper lip. "*Some*thing got hold of him."

"Ain't no doubt about that. Ole Lucky here got done in standin' off your bird."

"But are you sure it was my bird?" Douglas asked once again.

"You got the only red bird in these parts," the farmer said. "And I got me a henhouse full a this here." He stuck his free hand in his pocket and withdrew a sleek rust feather. "Only way to be sure's to check out your bird. My bet is he's missin' a few of these here." The farmer grinned. "That probably ain't all he's missin'."

Douglas ran his fingers through the copper wave of hair cresting his head and squashed it flat. "Look, would you like to step inside? Join us for a cup of coffee?'' His green eyes, floating on the surface of his face like two olives in a Martini, turned mournfully toward the house. The rerun would be over before this business was concluded.

"No, thank you kindly. I wouldn't want to drip no blood on your rug or nothin' like that. But I'd sure like to take a look at that big red a yours out back.''

As the three of us walked out toward the henhouse, Douglas said, "I really don't think Rusty's capable of. . .'' His chin bobbed in the dead rooster's direction. "But if he did it, naturally I'll replace your bird.''

"I didn't come here to cause you no trouble.'' The farmer wiped stray tobacco spittle from the corner of his thin lips onto the back of his hand. "But Lucky here wasn't no ordinary bird.''

Douglas gave me a sidelong glance. We both suspected that the farmer, to inflate the price of a replacement, would enlarge on Lucky's virtues.

We had reached the barnyard gravel, a ring enclosed on three sides by a crumbling split rail fence. The fourth side led directly into a dilapidated henhouse. Its open weathered doors hung askew on their hinges. Two dirty white chickens and one lame blonde hobbled about, occasionally pecking at the corn-poor ground.

"That where you lock 'em up at night?'' The farmer pointed at the henhouse with his chin.

Douglas and I exchanged glances.

"I don't lock them up at all,'' said Douglas. "It's against my principles.''

The farmer sucked thoughtfully at his teeth. "You oughta lock your big red in the henhouse,'' he said simply. His sudden grin revealed a crooked hedge of stained brown teeth. "Won't hurt your egg trade none, either.''

Just then Rusty, red gold, sovereign and impassive, emerged from the henhouse and moved rhythmically across the yard.

"Well, there he is,'' said Douglas. "I'll go get him for you.''

Amused, the farmer watched Douglas' vain attempts to catch the cock. Soon Douglas, out of breath and subsiding against the wooden railing, withdrew a handkerchief and wiped off the back of his neck.

"Here," said the farmer suddenly. He thrust the dead bird at Douglas' mid-section and slipped through the rails into the enclosed yard. Arms spreadeagled, he swooped down. Snatched up the lame blonde hen. And winked. "Easier to git, and with one a these here, you can catch all a them big fellers you want." Using the hen as a lure, the farmer soon had Rusty by the throat. Immediately, he released the hen.

"Don't hurt him!" Douglas cried.

"Let's have a looksee here," the farmer said, stroking Rusty's comb and cooing to help calm him down. "He's a big 'un, he is." His fingers plied the puffed up cock for telltale signs of recent war. "It's him, all right," he said. "Just lookie here."

Douglas gave a perfunctory glance and nodded. Despite his tall muscular frame, even taller than mine, Douglas was too sensitive to kill and dress his own chickens. I had no stomach for it either, claiming poor vision as an excuse.

"His comb's all mussed up too, see?" said the farmer. He held out a bedraggled piece of flesh that only yesterday had crowned Rusty's unblemished glory. "Have to cut that down some anyhow," the farmer muttered.

"Cut what down?" Douglas frowned. "What for?"

"First thing they go for in a fight's the comb." The farmer shook his head in disbelief. "Comb big as this 'n he still done ole Lucky in. Look at them spurs." He pointed to some spiny growths on Rusty's legs. Obediently, Douglas and I looked, but when our eyes met briefly, I knew Douglas was still wondering how much all this was going to cost. The farmer wheeled about and said, "Gimme that thing."

Douglas gladly handed him the hapless Lucky. The farmer, one arm around Rusty's warm and beating breast, the other hand around Lucky's dead neck, thrust Lucky into Rusty's face, waving him wildly back and forth.

Rusty tensed.

His pink eyes quickened with excitement.

The farmer, on his haunches, holding both birds bare inches apart, began to crow and hop on the heels of his muddy boots. Rusty's wings beat out a futile flap as he struggled to hook his rival of the night before. The farmer cackled away, hugely enjoying what he took to be a test of Rusty's mettle. Soon the whole barnyard was fluttering frantically to the tune of Rusty's and the farmer's shrill duet.

"Won't that hurt him?" Douglas cried out over the din.

"Who, *him*?" the farmer shouted back, breaking off his raucous squawking. "Na-a-h. He *likes* it. Don't you, you red devil, you." He held Lucky's corpse in front of his own face, a black feathery mask through which his challenge echoed as, with feints and sudden thrusts, he danced around the crazed live bird. Rusty trembled, straining to respond against the collar of the farmer's fingers to the farmer's eerie dance.

The farmer, noting distaste on our faces or perhaps simply grown tired, tossed Lucky to the ground. With his free hand, he took some pellets from his pocket. Pinching Rusty's cheeks with thumb and forefinger, he poked them down his throat.

"Ain't never seen the bird yet could resist these here."

Eyes half closed, he alternated stroking Rusty's breast with feeding him pellets. Rusty ceased to struggle. His squawks diminished to a snoring purr as he gave himself over to the farmer's fondling. When the farmer opened his fist to release him, Rusty did not move. Then suddenly exploding into a red blur, he flew over to where the dead bird had landed moments before. In jerking silent movie motion, as if to secure his conquest of the night before, his beak drove hard, over and over, into the black bird.

Douglas and I watched uneasily. When Rusty plunged his beak deep into Lucky's eye, I looked away. When I looked back,

Douglas was still staring as if transfixed. Bits of glazed pink matter hung down from his beak as, puffy-chested and sated at last, Rusty paced off the barnyard. The farmer, hands on hips and grinning broadly, watched Rusty's proud triumphal march among the indifferent chickens. "Jesus," muttered Douglas. "Jesus Christ."

"So that's the origin of the term *coxcomb*," I remarked, avoiding looking at Lucky's dark pocked remains. Rusty, meanwhile, seemed transformed. No more the backyard rooster, he hectored about, head high, exalted. The farmer watched him with a measuring eye. Suddenly he turned to Douglas.

"How much you want for him?"

Douglas was caught off guard. "For *my* bird?"

"That there is your bird, ain't it?"

Douglas nodded.

"Well, he jus' killed my prize game cock and you said you was willin' to discuss replacements. Now, don't go namin' me no fancy price 'cause he already done my champion in. I reckon that makes him worth Lucky's value, plus some. Now, jus' what do you think that plus some's worth?"

Douglas hunched his shoulders. "I thought cockfighting was illegal in Washington state." He knew perfectly well it was.

"Well, now, let's put it this way." The farmer sucked at his front teeth. "The county deputy owns the best fightin' bird in the Basin."

Douglas glanced over at what was left of Lucky. "I'll have to give it some thought."

"Sure would like to have him. He's got the biggest natural spurs I ever seen on any bird. With gaffs on 'em, he'll cut the deputy's Snow White to pieces. Snow White never could do to my Lucky what this here big red done."

We turned back toward the house. Douglas, grown thoughtful since the farmer's offer, suddenly said, "Oh, hey. Don't forget Lucky."

The farmer did not so much as look back. "Don't you worry

none about him. What the dogs don't git, the birds'll pick plumb clean.''

We reached the front porch of the house. The farmer took a pencil and small pad from his overalls pocket and scribbled out a number. "Gimme a call," he said, "when you're ready to talk business."

Douglas and I walked into the house and pulled our chairs up to the flashing screen. We had neglected to turn off the set.

"What's a gaff anyway?" Douglas wanted to know.

"I think it's a blade of some sort," I said.

Douglas made a face and turned his gaze from the flickering screen. "A blade?"

I nodded. "They attach them to the game cocks' legs before they send them in to battle. Ever seen a cockfight?"

Douglas shook his head.

"I went once," I said. "It got pretty bloody."

Douglas tugged absently at his wayward brows. "Sounds primitive as hell to me."

A roar from the crowd forced our attention to the screen.

"What round is this?" Douglas asked.

"I think this was the eighth. They didn't stop it until the eleventh."

"Get him, you chickenshit!" cried Douglas at the same moment someone knocked on the door.

This time it was a woman.

She too wanted to speak with the owner of the rooster who'd killed Sam Mitchell's prize game cock the night before. Annoyed at yet another interruption, Douglas nonetheless came to the door. Duty, no doubt, led him once more to the barnyard where he remained with the woman for some minutes before returning to the house alone.

"What was that all about?" I asked.

Douglas shut the door behind him with his foot. "She wants to buy Rusty too."

"What for? For cockfighting?"

Douglas shook his head. "For egg-laying. Says he'd make a great stud for her hens. Says his talents are wasted on a small time, run down chickenhouse like mine."

Douglas sank into the overstuffed armchair and clicked his tongue. "Seems all you have to do around here to impress the natives is kill something." He stretched his long legs out over the cable spool he used as both an Ottoman and a table. "I missed it again, didn't I."

I glanced at the screen, aflutter with activity as the seconds clustered round the fallen champion in a vain effort to revive him. His eye, invisible behind a mass of crushed pink pulp, oozed red and yellow matter down his battered cheeks. "'Fraid so," I said. "You owe me fifteen bucks."

"Shit," Douglas said.

"They might rerun it again later."

Douglas took a sip of cold coffee and made a face.

"You going to sell him?" I asked.

I'd been a fool to doubt him. He didn't even pause.

"No way."

"Not even for a good price?"

"Hell, no!" He punched the "Off" button with the toe of his bare foot, instantly converting the set into an unseeing black eye. "You know exploiting animals is against my principles."

Sherry Sue Sigler
Lawrence, KS

The Dying Senses

Merely existing
souls under an anvil
                    dying
Iron overlaid hearts
Past enjoyment of watching the spring colt;
relaxing moments of a cat stretched near
hearth of blazing fireplace
No longer can we smell coffee brewing;
taste the coffee bite
Gone are sweet whisperings of love
ferrous compound
minus energy to withdraw.

— ★ —

Rich Youmans
Lakewood, NJ

Labor Day, Long Beach Island

Bay of cold stars. . .
the causeway bridge
studded with headlights

Arpine Konyalian Grenier
Pasadena, CA

Under The Spell Of Time

Mounds scattered
on the skirts of Ararat
monastic mounds. . .beneath
their stone coloured silence
numerous tablets are described, interrupting
the peaceful monotony of green grass
they carry inscriptions of the myth of the deluge
of my forefathers, the ritual they performed
through aeons, to survive

They chose a female
cleansed and beautified her insides
programmed the crevices of her mind
and adorned her with the fruits of earth
the laminated praise. . that poured
out of their doubtful and agonized mouths. . .
when the rains started, they
entered her womb. . . like fetuses
they layed in its caressing fluids
oblivious to placental inscriptions
masturbating with them, consumating. .
blind with spirits, deaf to the echoes
of the voice in its pitch folds
the distant, desert voice
of grace

When the flood was over, they
slipped out, pushed by the thrust
of time, commenced performing
the solution of seconds, offered
hecatombs to the gods, prepared
multifaceted prayer sticks, with

colourful designs and intricate carvings
contaminated with abortive connotations
forever deaf to the nocturnal gong. . .
bloated prayer sticks, floating
on high waters, preserved
by the diluted brine
of the Dead Sea

There were also those
few amoeboid creatures
that fondled the placental folds
memorized their symbols and graphics. . .
when the flood was over, they stepped
out with a whimper
arched their vertebrae perpendicular
to the gods, overwhelmed at first
by the fresh green and blue, fluttering
with the pain of loneliness, haunted
by the images of their infantile nest
the memory of comfort
behind their ancient masks. . .
until they felt ground
under their feet, the majestic
folds of Mother Ararat
they offered no sacrifice, rather
began to inscribe the new
and transcribe the old

It was the gift of gods
to those that claimed
the will to describe

Joy Keiser Cochran
Midwest City, OK

Mabel Keiser

I was only a one-year-old
Who was dropped like a dolly.
My folks thought I was dead.
The funeral was in process,
I raised my head. But,
In five years my struggle
For life was over. No
More time, six years of
Life was enough for me.
I was no longer able to
Carry the load of Cerebral
Palsy. Six short years.
I couldn't play. So I
Faded into nothingness. Leaving
My brother to carry on
My name. Memories of Germany.
Memories of America now.
And the Keenapocamoca
River. In South Whitley
Indiana. Eel to you.

Jeanne Shannon
Albuquerque, NM

Tell Me How The Stars Looked In That Country

"It was so good to see you again last summer,
and talk about old times, old songs."

Blandish me with roses

Sing me old griefs
on the road to Cuzco

Whisper of green verandas,
and seabirds
rasping the air
under the palm leaves

Tell me of girls,
slim as the stems of lilies,
beguiling you
while stars drowned in warm rain

Give me back violets,
amazements,
and the white
hardness of the moon

Bernard Forer
Sarasota, FL

Snake In The Grass

Elusive beast, I know that you are there.
I've seen your tail
Undulating like a black whip
Traversing the sparse grass toward your hideaway.

Was it you or your cousin
That I encountered on the backyard lawn last month?
Your tongue darted in and out
As a signal of danger.
You dared me and fled me at the same time.
Threat and fear made a delicate balance
As you departed with amazing speed,
All forty inches of you,
Into the gathering dusk of the bushes.

But now I have glimpsed you
Moving like silent challenge to the right of my front stoop.
You are black.
I see no deadly patterns of yellow and crimson.
I do not believe that you will harm me.
Perhaps my presence
Has menaced you in your relentless search for game.
Do not be afraid, you thin slithering whip.
I cede you your roost in the thick bushes near the tired
              palm tree
That shades our kitchen.
Your empire is yours.
You may rule unafraid.

My main opponents are human snakes.
They are the brutes in expensive suits
Who menace me far more than you.

Virginia E. Smith
Laguna Hills, CA

Monet's Train On A Countryside 1870 *

In toy-like, see-through cars
they have traveled
for a pastoral outing.
The locomotive, unseen
save for trailing smoke,
whitstles atop an embankment.

Women with parasols
and a pink-frocked child
stroll on the grass.
Others have moved to the cool
of sheltering trees.

Monet recreates a day
in the country, uncorrupted
by speed and strain,
lost to time.

* Impressions and the French Landscape,
exhibit at the Los Angeles County Museum, 1984

DeWitt Clinton   *Michael Finley*
Shorewood, WI   *Minneapolis, MN*

Two Friends Say Goodbye

Cold rain, and water beads.

Two friends say goodbye.
You tug at the reins,
but the horse will not turn.

A ceremony, each
turns a special way, both
nodding & sorting —
detours, cutbacks, the two hairs cross.
There in the distance,
through the wrong end of the binoculars,
I see you waving.

We are the dull trees
that cannot touch without the
threat of ice.

A task, this horse, piling stones.
Who put these pitchforks in the sky?

A voice, a drive through upper rains
and winds that mostly stay.

Hesitant to say goodbye,
hesitant to begin alone.

The young dogs whine,
the old dogs hang their heads.

Katherine R. Whitten
Durham, NH

Eastern Promenade, Portland, Maine

On the rocky point
Cormorants spread wings to dry.
Wild roses, deep pink
Like those painted
On ancient Imari jars,
Sway in the faint salt breeze.
Clouds swirl after each other
In the deep azure sky,
As we walk beside the sea.
In the park, mothers
Wipe the noses of ungrateful children
And lovers embrace
Under a canopy of shade.

Our day almost over,
We dream of sailboats
To carry us away from these shores,
These roses, these crying children
Away from this life,
Where days like this one
Are as commonplace as cormorants
Spreading their wings to dry.

Elizabeth Rike
Brunswick, ME

The Cats Of Calandrino

A Tale from the Eleventh Night of The Decameron

You are to know, then, that Calandrino, of whom many stories have been told, being plagued greatly with mice on his farm outside Florence, provided himself with two cats to get rid of them. In this pursuit Gianni was unquestionably the better; for he was a big rough tiger cat, a fighter, whose approach to mousing was to rush wildly into the barn, pinning down and killing five or six mice before he began to eat them; which he did with great gusto, growling all the while. Fosco, on the other hand, a slim smooth brown cat, spent so long over each mouse, and would not cast an eye towards a second until he had delicately nibbled the first down to its bones, that for every dozen Gianni killed he barely killed two.

Calendrino, after buying the cats and installing them in his barn, had paid them no more attention; so he did not know that Gianni did so much more than his share, or he would most certainly have got rid of Fosco, as not earning his keep. No, it was his wife, Monna Tessa, who took care of the cats, who gave them milk when there was any to spare and pulled out their ticks. They soon became her dearest companions, and the repository of all her secrets; for even a termagant may wish to have secrets from her husband. And the cats were excellent listeners, when well fed and held on a knee — particularly Fosco, with his long, smooth, wise-looking face; though neither of them ever spoke, to Monna Tessa or any human being, until the events which I am about to relate.

All in all, it was an idyllic life for the two cats; but it did happen once that their lives were threatened, and that they only escaped by the utmost exercise of wit. The matter began one night when Bruno and Buffalmacco, who lived nearby and whom Calandrino counted as his dearest friends, though they had played him many a dire trick, were dining at the house of a priest. As they drank their wine Bruno brought up the subject of a fair which the two of them were planning to attend on the morrow.

"It saddens me, my friend" said the priest, "to hear you speak of such things, when I think of all the sins that are committed every time a fair is held."

"Yes, that's the only problem," Buffalmacco said; "every time I go to a fair, there is the long, dull confession and the penance at the end of it."

"These confessions are by no means dull to hear," replied the priest; "but on the other hand, I think I can help you out of this difficulty." His two guests stopped eating — at which pursuit Bruno in particular rivalled the cat Gianni in eagerness of appetite — and demanded with one voice to know how.

"Simply by absolving you in advance," the priest said. "Confess to me that you expect to sin grievously at the fair, and that you are already heartily sorry. I can give you no penance since you have yet committed no sin, but I will absolve you."

Bruno and Buffalmacco began to get down on their knees at once, but "Stop," said the priest, "not quite so fast; I will require some payment for this service, which you must admit is rather extraordinary. First, since you have dined at my table three of the past four nights, you must serve me a breakfast tomorrow, which must include a brace of good fat capons, and the best wine." His guests sat back in their chairs, glancing at each other; neither wishing to be the first to agree to this.

"And also," went on the priest, "I am having a cloak made for myself of cat skin, which it is well known is the softest and finest of furs, as well as the most varied in colour. It turns out that the stupid tailor did not provide himself with enough skin to start with; so the second part of your payment will be to bring me two cat skins, the most beautiful you can find."

"That's easy enough," said Buffalmacco; "Calandrino has two cats, who are supposed to keep his mice down; but I think they'd be more useful in your cloak. I'll set my dogs on them, while

Bruno here busies himself about preparing a fine meal for you.''

So it was agreed, and they parted; and no sooner had they left the dining room than Gianni, who had been lurking outside the window watching the birds, and had heard every word of their conversation, went racing back home like a streak of lightning. He found Fosco cleaning up a puddle of cream which the dairymaid had spilled, as was his tidy habit; and, dropping onto the stone floor of the dairy, panted out everything he had heard.

Fosco listened carefully, licking up the last drops of cream, and did not reply until it was gone and his whiskers were neat and well brushed. Then he said, "We must outwit them. Let us go to our bed in the barn, where we will be warm, and think."

But they had gone scarcely half the distance to the barn when there was a great noise of barking, and Buffalmacco's three dogs came rushing and leaping into the yard. The cats were so taken by surprise that they had no time to do anything but dash up the nearest tree; where Gianni turned and snarled at the dogs baying on the ground.

"Pay no attention to them," said Fosco, beginning to clean his whiskers all over again. "They will go away soon enough."

"Go away! In a minute I'll jump on them and tear them to pieces!" growled Gianni.

"Hush," Fosco admonished, and called down to the dogs, "Please, kind sirs, do go away and leave us alone!"

"And have you climbing down and escaping the minute we're gone? No thanks!" barked the biggest dog.

"But don't you know that cats can't climb down trees?" replied Fosco, in his most pathetic voice. "If you will only leave us in peace until morning we will have grown weak and fallen of our own accord, and you can just come back and pick us up."

The dogs stopped barking for a moment at that and looked at each other perplexed, unsure whether to believe Fosco; but he began to tell them tales of cats stranded in the tops of trees, who had at last fallen senseless to earth; and Gianni added the story of his great-uncle, who had constantly to be rescued from high places by men with ladders — so finally the dogs decided that it was true. Of course, Gianni's great-uncle had been notably feeble-minded, but the dogs were not to know that.

"All right then," the leader barked up to them at last. "We'll go away, but we'll be back at dawn!" And they loped off across the yard and home.

No sooner were they out of sight than Gianni ran to the edge of a branch and dropped to the ground, while Fosco followed the slower plan of inching down the tree-trunk backwards. Then they darted into the barn and curled up in their bed of straw, where they were soon fast asleep.

The next morning Bruno and Buffalmacco, having seen the cats properly treed but not having witnessed the ensuing conversation, returned to the tree to find no cats, but only the dogs, howling mournfully.

"Oh stupidest of canines!" shouted Buffalmacco, and began to whip them right then and there. Bruno joined in, and when the dogs had been thoroughly chastised, the two men declared to each other that they would catch the cats themselves. So they proceeded immediately to Calandrino's barn, taking great care that neither Calandrino nor anybody in his household knew that they were on his property; but for all their care, the cats heard their footsteps, and when looking out from their bed of straw they saw who was coming, at once they ascended to the second floor, and thence to the highest rafters.

Bruno was the first to discover where they had gone. "Come down from there, verminous cats!" he shouted, shaking a fist at them. Gianni's ears went back, but Fosco only licked a forepaw.

"You may have given my dogs the slip," Buffalmacco called up to them, "but we aren't that foolish. See this bag? I'm going to get a ladder right now and come after you, and then you'll find yourselves in trouble!"

"Meow," said Fosco. "Are we to understand that you think

we lied to your dogs?''

Bruno's mouth fell open and stayed that way, in his amaze-ment at hearing the cat speak, and Buffalmacco sat down hard, dropping his bag. Fosco stretched out on a beam, which was quite wide enough for him, and looked down on them amused. "You probably didn't know cats could talk, did you?'' They did not answer. "Nor could we, until last night," he continued; "talking to dogs does not count. There we were, my poor friend Gianni and I, stranded in the cold night twenty feet above the ground, when what do you think appeared to us? An angel, with shining face and many-coloured wings, and carried us down from the tree. Then he said — or rather sang, for he had the most beautiful voice I have ever heard — that as a reward for our patience, and in compensa-tion for what we had suffered, he would give us the power of speech. But alas, the angel is not here to rescue us now, so I fear we are stranded thoroughly this time.''

In the course of this speech Gianni had disappeared, obedient to some words which Fosco had spoken to him as they climbed to the rafters; but Bruno and Buffalmacco were far too astounded to notice that. In fact, it was some time before they could so much as speak, but at last Buffalmacco swallowed a few times and asked, "Where did the angel go?''

"Well," said Fosco, "you can be sure that there is no angel in this dark barn; but I did see him outside one of the windows later in the night. If you go to that window you may see if he is still about.'' And he began to walk delicately along the rafters, while Bruno and Buffalmacco followed on the floor below; both looking about them suspiciously, for this tale of an angel sounded a bit too much like one of the tricks they themselves had played on Calandrino. "And who knows,'' whispered Buffalmacco to his friend, "if the cat is really talking or if somebody is hidden in the barn, speaking for him?'' But as they approached one of the big square windows, which stood open, they both gasped; for there was a flurry of bright wings, dazzling in the sunshine.

"It is!" cried Bruno. "It is an angel!" He ran to the window, Buffalmacco close behind; and they were both so eager to see the angel that they fell right out of the window, which as I have mentioned was on the second floor.

Fosco stepped and jumped down to the floor, where he paused to look after them. And then Gianni joined him, and they stood laughing, watching Bruno and Buffalmacco struggle in the dung-heap where they had fallen, while Calandrino's big rooster squawked and fluttered his many-coloured wings nearby.

"He makes a fine angel, doesn't he?" said Fosco, as at last they ran off to Bruno's house, where a fine meal was cooking for the priest's breakfast. When the cook's back was turned it was but the work of a moment to steal the two fat roast capons that lay on the kitchen table, and then the cats dashed off, each with one in his mouth, to a quiet spot where they devoured the treat at their leisure.

When they had quite finished their meal, and their whiskers were cleaned to even Fosco's satisfaction, they returned to the barn to see how Bruno and Buffalmacco fared. They found them just managing to extricate themselves from the dung-heap, while Monna Tessa stood by with hands on hips, cursing them and commanding them to leave her barnyard forthwith. There was no sign of the rooster; having repaid his debt to the cats for allowing him to remain alive so long, of which debt Gianni had amiably reminded him, he had left off squawking and flying at their faces and had gone back to his hens.

"If that was an angel," Buffalmacco was saying, as he strove to rid himself of sundry unsavoury substances which yet clung to him, "it was one of the devil's; this might be purgatory itself!"

"Wait a minute!" exclaimed Bruno. "That is probably just what it is, purgatory itself; instead of being absolved ahead of time for our sins at the fair, we are being punished for them ahead of time, and we don't need that priest!"

"Then, I am glad purgatory is so close to home," said

Buffalmacco. "Anyway, I have had enough of cat-hunting, and so have my dogs!"

"And don't you ever come back!" Monna Tessa shouted after them as they stumbled out of the barnyard. "Cat-hunting indeed! I'll give you cat-hunting!"

Then Gianni and Fosco knew that they were safe from further persecution, and retired to their straw bed for a quiet nap.

Mary Ann Henn
St. Joseph, MN

A Miracle

Without knowing when
without precision
before the eye can verify
it comes it's there
more than sunlight
more than flowers
more than birds and bees
or leafing of the trees
it's all of these
and much much more
It's a dead world
winging once again
restored in spring

Nikolas Elevitch
Palisades, NY

Images With Purpose

Those puffy clouds
these sharp blades of yellow grass
high on a lonely hill
above the Connecticut farm houses
those red fences.

Wait-
look at the boy writing this.
look through his eyes.
look at this page with
black on it.
look off the page at yourself.

Click go the smooth rocks
that the boy holds squatting on the shore
they grate together
and make a sweeping sound
as he whips them out to sea.

Walt Franklin
Rexville, NY

At The Burial Site

Where mastodon and mammoth
hulked in shadow of the glacier,
where Lamoka fluted arrowheads
built fires for defense,
where Laurentians followed the migrations
knowing sources of the berry, fruit and spawn,
where Woodlanders discovered the use of clay
and the practicality of rounded houses,
where Hopewellians from Ohio settled
built their mounds for afterlife,
where ancestors of the Iroquois found leisure
and desire of possessions, war,
where the manufacture of projectiles flourished
during wartime, and ceramics during peace,
    it is summer solstice
by an old graveyard on the hill.
A woodchuck dens beneath a leaning stone
gray and weathered, indecipherable verse
for John and Dimmie Dutcher and
Barney— aged one year.
Above them: shaggy lilacs under maple trees.
From the west comes the call
of meadowlark and bobolink over timothy.
Eastward in the poplar grove
larvae of the gypsy moth cluster on bark
for shade, the few leaves left behind
now brown or black and curled.
    Like the single bigtooth aspen
still in leaf within the poplars,
I stand among them all, the peak of life
nothing of significance,
a potsherd or a bit of flint
for a moment flashing with sun.

Gail Rixen
Chokio, MN

Fossum

It's all gone now but the name,
sold out.
They came in on wooden wheels
and drove away on radials.
I just moved across the street
and sat down.

The new highway took business to bigger towns,
left us sitting like dolls on the empty streets-
dolls, who once fixed working parts
and put things in motion.

Sometimes when light comes in the shop window
and lands right there,
I can see Mabel in her rosy apron
or the stances of old friends.
Then I can smell the heat in the coals,
feel the weight of the hammer
and the metal that made our workings turn.

These days my new birdhouses swing in the trees,
pretty and empty, no good to anything.
Iron's dependable, keeps to its bounds.
Circumstance roughly pounds
the shape of my days.

Maria Jacketti
Hazleton, PA

Loki *

Great god of rabid
                bill collectors-
executor of Murphy's law-
You-worm-in-apple-grower,
rain-out,
          spoilsport, metabolic-
mischief-maker.
We bring you burnt offerings
antispectically sealed in vessels
of white ivory:
inside ghosts of steaming forests,
black, rotting crumbs of madgambler's delight,
ashes of the holocaust, still warm.

Loki,
so agile an actor,
chameleon-quick in your many personifications:
trickster,
          seducer,
                    huckster,
slickster,
          honeythroated divorce court
tychoon.
Without glint of warning, you nuzzle closer,
spray venom,
carpetbag the prey,
sink in your teeth.

Loki,
     almost benign sometimes:
sticky fly-in-ointment, zipper-jam,
patron of nonreturnable merchandise;

but also architect of the A-Bomb
and its more destructive offspring.
There is no joy in life that you will not
suck out
as you cultivate malignanacies, famine,
terinal lunacy.
Facing your dark masterworks,
older than Eden or the most distant deadstar,
we knit threadbare shields of optimism,
positive-think,
until you, with green glee, plink off our wings.

Loki,
     you wished this drought—
shit on my dreams,
ribboned these days with anguish.
But   be warned:
   I would lure you close to my heart;
whisper prayerful obscenities in your ear;
fill your veins with thermonuclear desire;
rip out your heart;
                  rape your sky-
and abandon you alive
               but dying
as you for pleasure,
          have left so many of us.

---

*
 In Norse mythology Loki is the trickster.

Keith McUmber
Minneapolis, MN

Winter Series,-#1

Winter lays claim to all she can wrench away
from life.

— ★ —

Keith McUmber
Minneapolis, MN

Winter Series,-#2

Winter is the deadness within the soul that
freezes all emotions within reach.

— ★ —

Keith McUmber
Minneapolis, MN

Winter Series,-#3

Winter is a cold driving force which pushes
you deep inside yourself to find a glow of
warmth.

Carol Adler
Pittsford, NY

Floridian Ice-Storm

For Ted Grieder

This is not a day for
crossing railroad tracks
or doing laundry

for the water pipes are frozen
and the power has been rationed
for heat thank God
and inside light.

So outside
the predawn streets are dark
all signals are off
and no towers are lit.

Nevertheless the trains
are still running
and one can hear planes
drilling through the iceblocked sky. . .

Imagine a rational God
wasting all that caution
on the everyday

and forgetting us in a crisis —
letting us die
anyway.

Surely *He* would not
take an arctic vacation. . . .

Bruce Bennett
Aurora, NY

The Anchor

We drag an anchor behind us.
It is attached to a long piece
of rope, and bumps and scrapes
over the earth.

We are held back by the
anchor. When it gets too
heavy, we take turns. That
way, although it's always
there, and someone's always
hauling it, it doesn't become
too much.

The children don't know
about the anchor. They say,
"Hurry up!" and "Why are we
going so slow?" We exchange
glances, and hold our tongue.
If they persist, we tell them
to be quiet; that we're going
as fast as we can.

Why mention the anchor?

Soon enough, soon enough,
they'll notice it.

Soon enough, they will
take their turn.

Joe Fuoco
Cranson, RI

Big Shot Rudy And The Lion

"When little boys grown patient at
last, weary,
Surrender their eyes immeasureably
to the night
The event will rage, terrific as
the sea;
Their bodies fill a crumbling room
with light"

Allen Tate
— Death of Little Boys

Big Shot Rudy looked at himself in the mirror and was not happy. He was big enough, bigger than he had a right to be for his seventeen years, but it wasn't the kind of bigness that made him happy.

He struck a pose in the mirror but it didn't convince him. He was certainly dressed for the occasion, for he had selected his clothing for the night of the big 'going down' very carefully, a new shirt, his trousers razor edge pleated, his shoes blinding in their shine, a leather coat he had worn but once. He was ready for whatever he and his cousin, the Lion might encounter. But he wasn't happy.

There was too much baby fat where there should have been muscle, a residue of childhood he should have discarded long ago. But he had been lazy, indulgent, spoiled as an only child without a father and a doting mother may be sometimes spoiled. He had always eaten too much and slept too much and never exercised enough, and now it had caught up with him to the extent he hated the way he looked. If he was going to be a part of something important and serious and if he was going to rub elbows with the big guys then he had to look considerably better than he looked. With his baby fat, his smooth chin, his freckles, and a tousled head of screaming red hair he was a boy-man comic reflection in his mirror.

"You look like Huckleberry Finn," Rudy said aloud, reproachfully. "A fat Huckleberry Finn."

He dismissed himself in the mirror and looked out of his second floor bedroom window to the shoulder of the hill a few hundred yards away. He narrowed his eyes and saw his friend getting into an automobile. Someone else was driving and Rudy recognized the car. Well, he thought, he's going to work hard tonight, Paul is, without your expert barking, he's going to work his butt off. He was aware of how Paul would be pushed tonight, Yelling his lungs out at the carnival, teasing customers into the tent where the big game was gaudily positioned.

This was their work. All summer, all fall Rudy and his friend, his 'blood brother' as he called him worked at carnivals throughout the region, often crossing state lines and getting deep into rural areas where people never saw much of anything in the summer but these itinerant carnivals. He and Paul alternately were ticket sellers, barkers, Rudy being the better barker by virtue of greater lung power, and all 'round carnival workers. It was never really dull, but it was never much of anything else, either, and this night, the night of the big 'going down' Rudy had cancelled the carnival, his friend, and even the girl. He had made a decision, and was holding to it. Even Paul's repeated calls and his warnings because he had some idea what was happening did not dissuade Rudy from his decision. It was his night and the Lion's night and there was going to be a big exchange and for the first time in his life he was going to be in the presence of the biggest of the big guys. The Lion had told him not to expect too much, but Rudy embellished it and made it a thing that excited him. He could barely keep his hands from shaking as he turned away from the window and reached in his coat pocket for the piece of paper the Lion had given him with the directions he was to take, and the appointed hour. He read the directions again for the hundreth time, still hoping he had read incorrectly. His hands shook wildly as he came to the place where the causeway was mentioned. It can't be, he thought. Why there? Why did the Lion have to make it their place of meeting? Because all his life, and particularly lately for some reason unknown to him Rudy was terrified of the causeway. It crossed the reservoir and was without light, and he had always been terrified of it. This was where he had to go because this was the first step of the night plans. There was nothing he could do about it. As he thought, he sat upon his bed and almost absently reached for the phone as it rang. He did not even extend a greeting, because he knew. The girl had been calling all afternoon, every fifteen minutes. He simply raised the receiver as easily as he would open a door.

"Don't go." It was the girl, of course. Rudy said nothing.

"Please don't do. Call Paul. It's not too late for the carnival."

"Yes, it's too late," Rudy said sullenly. He was tired of the whole business of excuses and restatements. He looked from his bed to the mirror and made a face at his reflection.

"Are you sure? Maybe it's not too late." The girl was persistent in the face of the truth. Rudy sighed.

"It is too late. I saw him leave in the car."

"Then I'll drive you. I'll take you." She was becoming desperate again. She had ended each phone call that way.

"No, you can't take me," Rudy said, his voice still very controlled, dull, and and almost sweetly apologetic. He could not take his eyes from his reflection. The way he sat, his belly overlapped his belt just enough to disgust him. This time he reproached himself and not the reflection as though it was someone else humiliating him.

It's not that you couldn't have done something about it, he said, but you were just lazy and didn't care. Now it's very important. Doesn't she realize it's for her as well. Oh, she loves you well enough and she doesn't seem to care about the way you look, but. . .

He was acutely aware of the girl's appreciative glances to other young men, even if she was faithful. It always bothered him but

more now as he took a long look at himself. He was getting older ,
and he was sick of being called a kid.

Behind all this, like a soft counterpoint was the girl's voice and
her pleas and he was only half hearing her. He glanced at his clock
and got up, holding the phone as if it were a prop without a real
connection. This would be absolutely her last phone call of the
night, he thought. Absolutely! He placed the receiver on the bed
and struck one final pose in his mirror. Then he raised the receiver
to his ear. There was only a persistent hum. So she gave up, he felt.
She'd be okay. She would be especially fine when she saw the
changes that would occur. Rudy had plans. With the money the
Lion was going to give him for doing absolutely nothing really but
for going along he would make changes. The Lion had promised
enough for a down payment on a car, even if it was a used one, and
there would be enough for a set of weights because that was part of
his whole reconstruction plan. It sure takes a lot to change your
life, he considered as he left the house and got into his faded
yellow- orange Cheverolet. This was going to the junk heap, he
thought. This was the first thing to go. Getting rid of the baby fat
and building himself into a monument of strength and beauty
would take a much longer time and it required a special discipline
so there was a lot for him to learn in changing himself. But he could
get rid of the old car easily enough and that was first in his plan of
things. Then there was something else, and he was certain that no
amount of money could ever secure that: a sense of importance, of
being with the big people, of knowing you were respected by the big
boys. You couldn't buy into that, he felt. You just had to be lucky
to be there. The Lion was his luck.

He counted himself poignantly lucky as he passed through the
town on his way toward the road leading nine miles to the reservoir
and the dreaded causeway. But he did not think about the causeway
at all as he passed the group bound it seemed to the buildings about
the intersection. They were his friends, schoolmates, milling about
the corners, standing with their backs against the buildings, their

boredom and restlessness evident in every gesture, in their lethargic wanderings. The nightly crew of nobodys, Rudy thought as he pressed his hand to the horn . He saluted them with contempt. He was very lucky indeed.

Up the steep hill toward a spread of farms and rolling fields Rudy drove, feeling the sensation of the climb, for he was climbing all the while. The vast watershed lay ahead in the late evening and he could see the darker clouds in the distance. He decided he would not slow but take the causeway all at once. That way he would not think about it and he would have no fear. His hands gripped the steering wheel and his determination was stromg, unyielding. Yet the car stopped. It stopped as if it possessed a will of its own, or some occult memory of a past fear. It just stopped where the road across the darkened reservoir began. Rudy felt his foot reflexively slam into the brake, and the jolt backward and forward. He could not take his hands from the wheel, nor could he raise his foot. The pressure in his leg was strong and he had the strange, frightening sensation of being paralyzed.

Now what was he to do, he asked himself. How do you get across? How do you get to the other side? You don't have Paul here to get you over there, to prod you, to lift your foot from the brake, to say all the things he would say to finally get you going.

Rudy remembered one of a series of encounters with the causeway and Paul's way of commanding that finally pushed him the few feet onto the asphalt that he needed to get going. All the encounters melted into one enormous fear. And he remembered Paul:

"Get that foot off, Rudy. Get it off."

But it wouldn't raise that easily. His eyes were as wide as half-dollars and they shone in the moonlight and Paul suppressed his laughter. He had to be very serious and in charge.

"I said get that foot off and hit the accelerator!"

Rudy tried. His foot wouldn't obey.

"Rudy, the carnival won't wait for us! Somebody else is going to take our place. You want that? You want that to happen?"

He never wanted that to happen of course, but there wasn't much he could do about it. Finally Paul took the only kind of action that he knew would get them moving. He quickly gripped Rudy's right leg and pried it from the break. Then he suddenly dropped it on the accelerator and screamed:

"Go! Go! Go!" And Rudy went. All at once. Too quickly. He nearly hit the stone with its bronze plaque commemorating the builder, some long forgotten Depression-era governor who no doubt, Rudy felt, never realized the fear the causeway would inspire.

In his mind he heard Paul's soft laughter, then his gale as they crossed. They crossed after the initial thrust very, very slowly.

"That was the longest Goddamndest mile I ever did travel," Paul shouted, laughing crazily at the other end, the safe end. Then he would say, as if to make Rudy less guilty, less ashamed for his fear:

"It's all right, pal, it's all right. It scares me too. Bet that's what it's like when you die. What do you think? You just get so scared and then let go and it's just slow moving and quiet, and you probably never see the end till you get there— just like crossing this road . You just crawl into nothing."

He never liked that. That was just too horrible to imagine: all that black, all that nothingness. He often asked himself, how do you just become nothing? How do you just stop? Doesn't seem real. Maybe it's best not to know it, not to ever see it happening, so that you don 't even know what you felt.

Now Rudy thought of all this, and imagined Paul next to him. He imagined Paul raising his leg, and he did raise it, and then dropping it upon the accelerator. It happened and he was in a jolt upon the road, starting like a shot, then slowing, and sweating his way, trembling his way across the black water on both sides. For it was very black now, and he could not see its limit. He thought of the things he would do with the money he would get from the Lion. that helped. He'd get rid of this heap and get started on his building program for his body and he would leave that group of aimless corner wanderers and find himself a very important place where he would be respected and no longer thought of as a big kid, bigger than he should be, baby-fat bigger.

He was on the other side. The car stopped, easily this time, and Rudy smiled at his conquest. So he had done it alone. That was a good sign, he felt. He had done it without Paul because he was certain that thinking about him did not do the whole job. The courage and strength had to come from him.

Now he felt in his pocket for the note, and by the light of a tiny compartment bulb he read the Lion's instructions. He knew the tree, the small dirt road, and he started the car and drove in the dark until he came to the place. The tree was a great, menacing thing that had lived very long and was dying. The wild summer storms had taken its heavy, ashen branches as if its arms had been broken, and it had been condemned by those who condemn such things to death. It was home to an assortment of insects and they had hollowed it so that it stood by tradition, and by little more. Next to it lay the dirt road that slithered between the trees. Rudy didn't know where it led. He had never walked its length. He parked and waited. He was definitely not getting out of the car.

The Lion startled him. He seemed to suddenly materialize at the window. He rapped on it and Rudy jumped. The Lion's face wore a strange, mischievous grin. He was both laughing at Rudy's fear and that he had made it: the Lion had had some reservations. He was glad now because he needed Rudy. He needed his bigness, nothing more. Oh, there was something else, but he didn't want to think about it. If the worst happened, then Rudy was to take the bags and bring them to a place where they would be exchanged for money. This is what he explained now as he sat next to Rudy.

"In case something happens. . ."

"You said nothing would happen."

"No, nothing is going to happen, but. . ."

"But what?"

"The extra stuff will be here. We're going to plant it here. The big tree will be the marker."

"Bury it?"

"We have to. If they're willing to go along, if they buy the story that I haven't collected, then we'll get rid of it, for a bigger profit. That's where you have to help."

"What do I have to do?"

"Take this."

It was another note. The Lion was going note crazy, Rudy felt. Everything has become a note. Now what the hell is this?

It was another address, with names, and a way to get there.

"You take the stuff there. You take it and you show it to this guy and everything will be okay."

"And where will you be?"

"By then? Who the hell knows." The Lion seemed resigned, said it in such an off-handed manner, as if it meant nothing. He seemed a little tired, slowing down as if he had been running all day.

Rudy didn't like the atmosphere. It wasn't the dark, but the feeling of somehting hollow, murky. He was getting scared and he didn't know why. Maybe it was a mistake. The girl was right and he should have listened to her, and Paul — well, he was probably better off barking at the carnival. At least he was sure of what he was doing.

The Lion, as if guessing Rudy's misgivings, slipped a small elastic bound roll into his pocket. Rudy was startled by the act.

"That's half," the Lion said. "You know, I don't have to give you anything now, but, well, what the hell, you came along, and you're my cousin, and . . ."

"I don't know," Rudy said, surprising himself. He felt the roll, it felt good, full, and with a promise of more, but he was shaking and he couldn't stop. He thought of all things he would do with the money but they weren't as exciting. There were just too many questions.

"Don't know what?" The Lion asked.

"Maybe. . ."

"Maybe what?"

Then Rudy did something he never dreamed he would ever do. It was the very last thing anyone would have expected. He tentatively extended the roll of money to the Lion

"What the hell is this?" The Lion shouted. His voice echoed over the water.

""I. . . I. . ."

"You what? You backin' out? You want to go? You CAN'T GO! It's too late. Put the money back!"

Rudy hesitated. He seemed to make a move to return the money to his pocket, but then he extended it again. The Lion was furious.

"Take the money, Rudy," he bellowed. Rudy sunk in his seat, turning his face away from the Lion. His right hand still extended the roll of money.

"Take the fuckin' money!" The Lion screamed with violence.

Rudy's arm dropped. There was no point to his persisting. He was in it now, whatever it was, to the very finish. The Lion wouldn't let him go.

"I need you along, Rudy," the Lion said calmly, making a different kind of appeal. "I really do need you along. You're very important to this. Look - it will take a few minutes. All that money for a few minutes."

Rudy nodded his head, returned the money to his pocket.

"Okay," the Lion said. "No sweat, Rudy. Easy thing. A snap. First we bury the bags. I put a shovel in a little clearing. Let's go."

They were out of the car and along the narrow dirt road that went by the ancient tree. Deep along the road Rudy followed the Lion until he turned and walked into an utterly black place that had few trees. There was a shovel on the ground and two small bags. Within the bags were other bags, tiny plastic bags, transparent, their contents a pure, unspotted white. Rudy took the shovel and dug until there was a hole deep enough for the bags. He buried them and the Lion then returned the sods and placed them so that the ground looked undisturbed. The Lion had hidden his carr off the asphalt road. It would stay hidden until they had returned. The Lion had decided upon this because he knew Rudy's car would be unknown to the men. It was simply an extra precaution he was taking.

For Rudy, the night was becoming stranger with each new development. He had never expected to be burying anything at all, and he certainly never thought he would be following the message upon another piece of paper— alone. He hoped it wouldn't come to that. He didn't want the responsibility of having to do anything without the Lion.

They had to return along the road of the causeway, but Rudy was less frightened the way back because he turned the wheel over to the Lion. It gave him a chance to look at the Lion while he drove, to really look at him.

He didn't look so awesome, Rudy mused. Not at all. Actually, too small for great things. But there he was, the Lion. That had nothing to do with courage, and in a way Rudy felt satisfied because courage wasn't the core of the Lion. He was the Lion because somebody just dropped the "e" from his surname and he *became* the Lion. Rudy felt a little more equal thinking about that. It meant to him you might become anything at all if you just dropped the right things along the way.

Within an hour they were there, stopping before a three story house on a busy, narrow street where all the tenement houses were the same and looked as if one set of blueprints had been used without variation. The Lion rolled down his window and looked up toward the windows of the third floor. He seemed apprehensive, and moved the car away from the house. He found an alley and parked it there . If they had to move quickly it was best the car wasn't seen at all. The Lion knew the area well. His business had been conducted here for a long time. Rudy felt a little confident because of that. But only a little.

In the hallway of the three tenement house he followed the Lion up the dark stairway, his heart pounding so that his ears felt they would pop with the beating . He was breathing so heavily that he felt dizzy. The climb was interminable. Finally, stopping on the last landing before a door he could see a faint yellow light penetrate the cracks in the door and spread beneath the doorway. He sucked in his breath and refused to breathe as the Lion rapped on the door. A woman opened the door. She did not smile but only left the door open and went down the stairs. Rudy had time to notice that she was very young, and suddenly he was in the room. The Lion gestured toward a corner near a window and without a word Rudy went across the room and glanced only once toward the little table at the far end, two men behind it, a little lamp the only light, the rest of the room dark, and absolutely empty. Rudy looked out the window to the street below. He didn't want to know what was going on. He wanted to pretend he wasn't there at all. He thought of the girl and it didn't work, and he thought of Paul and that didn't work either. He heard voices and then they grew louder, and although he didn't want to look he had to! There was the Lion on one side of the table and the men looking at him without expression and the Lion talking a blue streak, as fast as he could. Upon the table were little piles of money, tied with elastic. Then they were all very angry, all arguing, and Rudy, trembling turned away. Somewhere in all of the sounds of the voices came the subtle hiss like the exhaling of a breath, then another. The voices stopped and Rudy turned to face the scene. The Lion was on the floor, and a stream of blood was moving across the floor-boards. The blood looked purple and was coming from his head. Rudy slid into the shadows of the corner. Then he felt himself sinking as if he was attempting to be absorbed by the shadows without realizing it; he wanted to disappear.

He heard again the voices of the two men and they were glancing in his direction. One of them held a large gun, or a gun that looked larger because of something placed over its barrel. He walked toward Rudy and Rudy closed his eyes. He had seen the expression in the man's face, and he did not like what he saw.

Philip Wexler
Bethesda, MD

Normalcy

the emblem of sanity is
embossed on your cloth of conformity
which is an outward profession
of the very opposite you embody.
to the community it is the unknowable.
just occasionally the hidden earth
beneath the cloth sprouts
a seedling which it cannot hide
and the community takes it as
a peculiarity which is
perhaps an accident or
a lapse in a mentality
which is very sane.
they would never guess
that this seedling is no mutant
but an outgrowth of
the dark aberration
which is no emblem but
the substance and foundation,
which rests with open eyes behind
the cloth of conformity,
and seeps out in the evenings
unrecognized in its own mileu.

F. Hayes Scribner
Newbury Park, CA

Alive: Again

at first light,
with her pressed warm against me,

 I awaken
 to a dream,
 and lay there,
 reliving yesterday on the hillside, with all the world green
 around us, while far below in the valley a hawk
 circled silently above the trees by the lake and,
 surrounding us like slow-moving ocean waves, the tall,
 seed-heavy grass rustled softly in the warm April breeze,

—and us,

 aglow after years of darkness, touching,

 reaching, whispering insane things to one another,

 laughing: *Alive!*

. . .Stirring now, she's awakening, and
I can feel the excitement begin to grow
as I await the magic of her eyes.

Cheryl D. Bynum
Macclesfield, NC

Two Smiles In Winter

Two smiles and a walk in the park,
They held hands and cried.
Ectasy had come. And gone.
The Poets had lied.
Baby's breath, daffodils and mums.
All fresh and alive.
All dead and all gone.

Winter had left its mark
Everything beautiful and alive was dying,
No. Everything had died.
A single smile and a walk in the park
Memories enveloped and suffocated her.
She stood by the pond and cried.
Here it had begun and here it had died.

Charles Lance Fox
Augusta, ME

Lakewood Reflections

The park bench holds love
carved deep in wood
more permanent than the unavailing heart

> "Always I love you
> Rosa 78"

Be still, be quiet, become
October's ceremony of the dying
leaves radiant Indian blankets
ignite a stick of melancholy incense
and with contests of fire colors
arouses vague aromatic pleasures
another park, another age
another lover's reverie

Piano notes here from a side street window
linger briefly in delicate symphony
with the wind and a million blazing palettes
painting a divine memory on the senses
of those who travel slow.

Invitations too, to test a grand illusion
to walk among inverted trees
and clouds hung from a solid sky
glazed in still water below

A holy man appears on the hill above me
and by his deep presence invokes cabalic expectations
a dark silo of fermented knowledge, bearded
and sobering in the animated row of squirrels
he stands with ancient book clasped in veins

assessing my solitude, my purpose
all blessings are accepted here
I sense favor in the air

This tender heart of a tough town;
five or ten minute walk-to-vacation
this strip of paradise
around whose lovely shores
horse and buggy millionaires
clatter only in aging memories
was mine today

Now the bells of St. Mary peal immaculate
and crowd time is approaching
hurling noise and stealing space
and I'm reminded
love-times-two calls me home

— ★ —

Rich Youmans
Lakewood, NJ

Over Housing Tracts

Over housing tracts
Marlboro Man staring
at the desert horizon

Louise Jaffe
Brooklyn, NY

Sometimes After Summer Rain

Sometimes after summer rain
You waken
And the new day wears the beaming face
Of summer's end
And sun.
Then you begin to think
That last night's questions
And tangled messages
Dangling in the sweaty air
After humid lusts
and gusty couplings
Have all been washed away.
For a smileful while
Your breathing
And dreaming
Gleam with new-found ease
And your heart
Can almost fly
In the morning winds
And your words can almost purr
"If he grows overbold
Feels me a weariness
And icily recites
'Though it was nice
I find I do not need you anymore'
I will not wince
Or care."
Sometimes after summer rain
Before the next clouding
Life feels that way
For then.

Lydia Rand
Mendocino, CA

Voices

"Do you know what the cat lady did to-day?"
"What?"
"She sat for hours in front of Mendosa's
wearing
her new free box clothes, some of mine in fact.
I tossed them in there yesterday,
on her, they were too small.
She looked so weird! That with her lips all painted black,
and wearing a moustache and black freckles on her face. . .
  "She always does that, she thinks she is a cat!"
  "I know but this time, there was more! She was with her huge
orange cat, the one she takes everywhere with her.
Well! You know what? She patted and caressed that cat for hours
and each time it opened
its mouth
to yawn or meow,
she
frenched it! What a freak!"

At he foot of the High School stands
a shaky water tower.
The cat lady lives there.
Coming back home one night she wrecked
what was left
of her car
running into
what was left of the door.

The afternoon is slipping into harvest.
The sun drinks all visible ocean.
The cat lady scoops it up and brings it
to her mouth.
Many times it passes through her teeth as she laughs,
and laughs to herself.
Not to herself!
In a half circle around her
three sitting cats are laughing with her!

G.D. Richards
Jacksonville, AL

Teeth

A row of teeth
along a downed branch.
What has bitten so terribly, then
couldn't let go?

But no: I see
it is the wood
that has grown teeth—
gnawing,
devouring itself . . .

devouring all that has failed
its imagination.

Debora J. Bork
Caledonia, NY

Parrot Shirt

The world is flat. I walk and walk, wanting to reach the edge. There doesn't seem to be an easier way out, so I have decided: when I get there, I will jump. On the way, I most often meet people that encourage me (without knowing) on toward that goal. Rarely, there is someone who wants me to stay, but their feelings never last. Sometimes, I really want them to, but after awhile, I learn that it hurts more to hope. Ultimately, hopes are dashed.

I am intelligent, maybe too much so. If I didn't think so much perhaps I'd be happier. As I walk on toward the edge, words or phrases start to repeat themselves in beat with my steps, over and over. I can't stop them once they start. Something drastic has to happen to make my attention shift. It drives me crazy and I can't think of anything else. The phrases start to speed up and I walk faster and faster and then my mind goes faster, and words start to trip over themselves and I'm almost running. I don't know which happens first but it doesn't matter. I try to run from the repetition, but I can't.

Yesterday I stopped in a 7-Eleven and asked for a pack of Camel straights. The woman behind the counter looked at me like I was from the moon. I had to repeat myself and she snapped back at me that she'd heard me the first time. She had on a black short-sleeved blouse with brightly colored parrots on it; it was a nice blouse, cut sharply between her breasts. I thought about the blouse as I left the store, pausing on the steps to light a cigarette from my new pack. I always liked new packs of cigarettes. It was early morning, the sun had just started (new pack of cigarettes/cut sharp a parrot shirt) to light the sky. It was going to be a beautiful day, warm but not too warm, hazy, sleepy.

I hadn't been sleeping well lately and I figured it was the new, long days of walking and the changing seasons. I had laid low in a small town in Tennessee over the winter and this was the third day of my second week on the road. I was having a hard time (new pack cigarettes/cut sharp parrot shirt) adjusting this year. I hadn't wanted to leave Tennessee. The school where I was teaching was small and my peers there had seemed to appreciate - even like - me. There had been some great parties (new pack cigarettes/cut sharp parrot shirt) and a woman, an English instructor, who had taken the lonely edge off many of my weekends. (new pack cigarettes/cut sharp parrot shirt)

I was beginning to walk quite fast, not really knowing my direction. I reached for another cigarette (new pack cigarettes) and two fell to the ground as I fumbled with the pack. I didn't stop to pick them up. The trees were going by in a blur, I wasn't sure that it was I that was creating the movement anymore. (new pack cigarettes) It seemed like I was running now, air pushed my hair back, whistling, I heard it (cut sharp) whistle. My vision was blocked out suddenly, all was black but there was color, small (parrot shirt) spots of color.

I taught well. I actually enjoyed teaching because I loved to write and wanted to share that love with other people. The kids always had good things to say in their evaluations. I'd even had students come to see me at the end of the year and ask me to stay. I could never tell them why I had to move, it was a personal thing. I suppose, in the end, they thought I was just an eccentric old artist that had to move on. This year it hadn't been the students as much as that English instructor. She was a tough girl, but even she got teary when I told her I was leaving. It made me think twice about it, we had some good times. But ultimately, I knew she didn't care, it wouldn't last. I had to keep walking.

I was so tired. It took awhile each spring, maybe a month,

before I could walk all day without being tired. I had vague memories of places I had passed during the day but I could never clearly describe them. Often, writing in my journal each night, words would flow beyond any conscious control. I would read them later and wonder what they meant. They were usually disturbing somehow, but I couldn't put my finger on how or why.

May 23, 1984

It seems that I'm getting closer. Dreamt about a storm last night, a storm of bright colors, in bits. The sky was full of color and it swirled and swirled and I watched for hours (it seemed). Smoke filled the air, then the storm came down around my head, roaring but quiet, a storm of brightly colored feathers. It seemed so familiar.

I finally came to a fork in the road, one that I sensed was different and I knew this was it: my last decision. The road that went northeast was cool and tree lined as far as I could see, which wasn't very far, since the road curved off quickly. It looked inviting. The road east opened up to a meadow straight ahead, cutting through tall grasses, brightly lit, hot. I sat down and ate an apple that I had bought awhile back, savoring it and my decision. I threw my apple core across the road, listening for it to drop. Leaves rustled as it passed through, everything slowed down to an infinite slowness. The core never hit the ground. I pondered this for what seemed a long time, then decided it was time to go. I started walking into the meadow. The path was soft and I walked noiselessly. I heard sound to the sides of me but I ignored them. They were probably apple cores falling or parrots flying. Ahead, I saw a wall of mist rising. I noticed for a second that it shouldn't be: the sun was hot, it was mid-afternoon. I didn't care. I entered into the mist, it was instantly cool and dark. (new pack cigarettes/cut sharp -) There was no time to congratulate myself on knowing the truth. I jumped.

Ann Chernow
Westport, CT

Epitaph

Born in steerage
Rosie grew up and became a Flapper;
Her steno job paid well
She gave her momma five dollars a week
And spent the rest on ciggies and clothes.
Her sisters watched her cavort nightly
With her many beaux, gathered around the rented piano;
Rosie married the one with the best personality
He was the poorest.
The great dream failed for Rosie,
Her son was a disappointment
Her husband never 'improved himself';
They remained in a tenement, always just managing.
Growing old, Rosie had a stroke,
No one would care for her.
She was sent to a charity home where she
Died in storage.

Ron Maggiano
San Diego, CA

Lichen

sadness is a creeping lichen
crawling into rocky crevices
curving into every corner
where there is no room

light's feeble fingers
cannot probe every facet
nor rain or snow evict
the fungus from the shallow
which sadness calls home

who knows
when the lichen starts
where the germ is from
how the color comes
for lichen has no explanation

these fossils are fixed
on granite's face
covered as your brow too
is etched in sadness

lichen is your mask

lichen is your joy
still your celebration
your silent ecstasy
covering the bareness

i have ruined my hands
trying to pry the lichen
from your forehead

is there some other tool

Susan A. Katz
Monsey, NY

Other Lives

A thousand times
a thousand lives
linger on this lip
of memory believing
themselves whole.

I have drifted to this shore
before, the scrabbled sand
is like a nest that holds
the scent of birth, the sky
pinned to itself by stars
that relieve themselves ·
of light, the wind blowing
my name.

I cannot count the times
I've stumbled
on myself, come back
through tunnels, through
trails overgrown with shadow
through water that moved
without intention
from shore to shore.

We move, holding ourselves
together with what we label
dreams, toward horizons,
toward crests that loom beyond
the flight of birds muttering
small relevancies as though
we owe a debt we cannot pay.

And in the end, the fusion
of land and sky, is always just
beyond our reach, the mountains
clamor toward a sky that swallows
them in mist, oceans heeding
the pull of gravity carry us
like seeds back
to beginnings. . .

       toward silent lives
       that are our own;
       toward other lives
       that leave us
       less than whole.

— ★ —

Vera Lee Baker
Claremore, OK

To Turn Again

I would give up this hard-earned wisdom
And turn back through the now-closed door
To see once again through my Genesis eyes
To feel with young Eden senses
The pure fresh silk of new love

I have put my hand to the plow
And will not look back —
But wild violets flew
From under my lawn mower today
Spreading my heart in blue tatters

Adam D. Fisher
Stony Brook, NY

Cast Of Wedding Characters

The doorman
in red and black cutaway
salutes the bride, packing
in her mouth, face swollen
from root canal.
Her father's belly
strains against
his ruffled, pink shirt.
The groom, who needs a haircut,
stands inside on thick carpet
under chrome and glass chandeliers.
Waiters change in the Men's Room
from sneaker and jeans
to red jackets, gold epaulets.
The Maitre d', with continental accent,
directs us
with polite condescension.
The Grand Hotel's white plastic runner
lies ready and torn.

Ross Staples
South Easton, MA

Two Cellar Holes In Maine

filled with rubble and brambles remain
of a Belgrade Lakes family farm.
The eighth generation, five sons strong,
left here in late nineteenth century,
joined the Maine exodus to Boston
to mix with European migrants
in search of the American dream.

As children they had watched nature's blows,
losing the horse through the ice,
crops to drought, fingers to frostbite
driving the ox team to Augusta,
uninsured house and barn to lightning.
Their widowed mother, strapped, sold the farm
for a pittance due the mortgagee.

These farm bred sons without a trade
chose rented, heated three deckers
with the full gamut of utilities
to log-splitting, well, outdoor privy—
steady pay as laborers, coachmen
instead of farmers' risky cash flow.

Some of their city bred grandchildren
trek to Maine, seek escape from stress,
fish, swim, ski, hike, bike, sail, picnic.
They wish that after lightning struck
their grandfathers had shaken their fists
at the sky, and yelled like John Paul Jones
on the floundering *Bon Homme Richard,*
"We have just begun to fight,"
or like the bombed-out Japanese
dug out the rubble, built anew,
but all the offspring find instead—
two cellar holes and a gorgeous view.

G.D. Richards
Jacksonville, AL

Heartwood

I stand in gray woods
staring at the ruins
of a common pine,
the top snapped off head high.

Around the base,
an untidy scattering
of bark slabs and weathered wood
like discarded notions.

Only the spire remains,
heartwood,
the color of . . .
fresh bread crust, I think,

but cracked and fissured
like new-turned
earth, seamed with rich shadows.

Heartwood—pure heartwood.
Who would flinch, dreaming
his life might come to this?

Evelyn Wexler
Bronx, NY

Van Gogh

The argument continues.
You know, the one about madness and
genius. It is a little known fact
that he was sane for many years.
He was Renoir at the time.

Room after room of saneness,
salons of sanity.
Sweet soft sanity. Meringues of sanity.

Soft shadows, cast by soft trees.
Soft buttocks sitting on soft hillocks.
Soft stones to avoid hurting soft feet of
Soft bathers using soft soap.

When he became Van Gogh,
he memorized the sun.
Staring into spiraling granite,
screaming writhing light,
he learned how some
Craziness can keep an artist
holy.

Small price:
An ear.
A life.

Carol Adler
Pittsford, NY

Round Trip Ticket

"They really are terrible people," said Lori, helping herself to another wedge of pecan pie. It was breakfast and Lori had just informed me that while overseas visiting her terrible relatives in Switzerland, my sister and brother-in-law, she had put on another ten pounds. Which totalled thirty plus, she said, that she had to get rid of. But she is 25, I reminded myself, and I was only her mother.

"First of all, Patricia is fat, grossly overweight, and she does nothing about it, she never stops eating. This pie is great, did you make it?"

"No, thanks, I mean no, I didn't. I don't bake anymore for just the two of us. Daddy remembered you like pecan pie."

"What do you mean 'the two of us'? It makes you sound old and lonely. God it's great to be home, I'm so exhausted, I hate to travel. But anyway I suppose I have to start looking for a job, I hope I don't find anything too soon."

"What do you have in mind?" I ventured, throwing away my melon rind.

"Well of course something that pays much better than minimum, and something that's not too exhausting . Do you have any cheese besides low-fat, or any whole milk? How can you eat that stuff, it's terrible tasting."

On other occasions when Lori had returned, I considered moving out of the house, finding a nice quiet apartment maybe near a lake so I could watch ducks and sailboats and lie on the beach. Well at least for ten minutes. I'm not much of a beach bum, but I do love to swim. Lori would be eating and sleeping here until she found her ideal job. At least Bobby and Janet would be away at college for the next four, five years. I could get a full-time job myself. In addition to my community volunteer work and course-auditing, that would keep me out of the house. And I could probably qualify at McDonald's, they always need help. Or I could take a position as a live-in babysitter.

"And Harold is so lazy, and he's also fat. You know, I think I have a prejudice against fat lazy people. I can't help myself, I just don't like them."

In the basement while running through the Swiss laundry and collecting the vacuum cleaner and dust cloths, I ruminated. You have been a good mother, I'd told myself when Lori graduated from Wellseley with a major in Psychology and the offer of a paid graduate fellowship at Harvard, which she had turned down.

You did bake cakes and pies, even when it was no one's birthday or Christmas or Thanksgiving. And you cleaned everyone's bedroom, emptied all the wastebaskets, even now you make beds and change the linen. But that's only because you can't tolerate dirty feet between dirty sheets.

I could go to the library every afternoon. And there were several to go to, once I finished reading through one, if I considered all the city and suburban branches. This could probably keep me preoccupied for more than a lifetime.

My dustcloth paused on the keys of the grand piano. I struck a major triad and modulated to a minor third. Was there any greater sin than mine? That was so great I dared not even confess it to myself? "You are a despicable human being," I said aloud, with the back of my hand wiping the sweat from my forehead. "And your punishment is this self-awareness in visable and largely tangible form, that you may be forced to reside with for the rest of your days." How Old Testament sounding, I thought, suddenly remembering I was low on water. Spring water. And Lori would be furious if she should open the food cupboard — chances were rather good that she would — and discover only food on the shelves. Lori would not drink anything but beer from a tap. It was fattening (tap *water*) because it made cellulite. And the reason why she had gained ten pounds in Switzerland was because of the impurities in the Swiss water.

You're afraid she will stand there in the middle of the kitchen her eyes blazing, her two fat feet planted firmly apart as she lifts her arm and points one of her fat fingers at you accusing you of shirking your shopping responsibilities. Aren't you? Aren't you?

When I last had the temerity to mention Diet Workshop Thinking Thin Feels Great Aerobic and Weight Watchers, Lori delivered a Phi Beta Kappa lecture on body language image-seeking and behavior modification. I knew already that it does not necessarily follow that fat people are jolly or happy or energetic. But I was ignorant about the fact that, if one loses weight, he/she would not necessarily be psychologically or in any other way, transformed. "Some people *like* to be fat, some people like to hide beneath layers of fat,"et cetera. "Furthermore," she claimed, citing statistics and various samplings of sophisticated studies that appeared in reliable journals and magazines, "there is not necessarily a correlation between energy input and caloric output, between metabolic body-types, hypothalmic motivation-visualization techniques, learned or unlearned, and the ability to lose weight."

My own observations, amateur as they are, have always led me to adopt a party line whose slogan was "Doing is Believing."

Losing weight, I'd learned, required work, and work was often a difficult "act", one that it did not seem too probable therefore, that a lazy, unmotivated person could accomplish.

Usually sex provided excellent motivation, I reasoned. Lori was not a lesbian, nor was she neuter as far as I knew. And she did score A-Plus in the department of other appetites. Although I knew there was possibly no correlation here either. Fat lazy men often made lousy lovers, the fat being an eating problem that was covering up the sex problem.

I dumped out the dozen roses I'd purchased to celebrate Lori's arrival and held my nose. Roses did not last as long as they used to, I thought. Or maybe it was I who was growing shorter-spanned-and-tempered, now seeing things like roses and college degrees myopically. The problem with men is, I continued my reverie, filling a bucket with Lestoil and water and getting down on my hands a n d knees on the kitchen floor, squeezing out the sponge; mostly they like thin women, even if they're fat themselves. "But maybe not all men," Lori had lectured me. "There are fat men who like fat women."

But here again: What kind of man in today's thin-conscious world would let himself go adipose unless he had glandular trouble? Job-seeking competition was fierce, I didn't have to remind myself. Lori was living proof. Bulging bellies were hardly tartar sauce for pin-striped suits.

"MOTHER!"

I stiffened and waited, a cold shiver shooting up my spine. "MOTHERRRRRR!" God if I did something else wrong, please have mercy, pity me, I prayed.

"Oh there you are, why do you always work so hard, I just had a strange thing happen to me, suddenly it came over me, Mother, how much I love you, how much I truly truly love you, and — don't stand up, that's OK, I won't walk where you just mopped. So I had to come and tell you. I had to tell you what a fantastic person you are, what a first-rate mother and human being. I mean after spending two ugly weeks with two ugly people, I feel so lucky, so grateful. I never fully realize what it means to have parents like you and Daddy until I'm away from home. Do you know what I mean? You're such a helluva special person, not only intelligent and accomplished, but a great companion. I like to talk to you, I enjoy being around you, I really do. I know I can always count on you to know what I'm saying and to listen to me. Do you know how few people listen in this world? Oh God, mother, you don't have to cry, I didn't mean to make you cry! Mother! Oh God, mother, stop bawling—!—

Lee Bridges
Amsterdam, The Netherlands

Intermezzo

The troubadour rhymes while crumbling facades of
Grave shawled senoras are beginning to look like
Ancient sculptures on mud splattered ravines

With haunting medieval chimes stealthily regurgitating
A chilling sense of infinitiveness as surging waves of
Blues pulsates towards grey deserting scenes

Diminuendos in recline

For sudden unheeded outbursts of naked excitement is
Dwindling into little trills controlled and released
with precisely the right sound

But there is wine

And memories of orange-red lights brighter twinkling
Heights and of promises and of promiscuities and of
Love songs filled with drama and of every regret

Of ever changing times though the movement drones on
With the flamenco dancers becoming exhausted and the
Cathedral clock striking out indignantly in old
Spanish town

Until the next set.

S. Axtell
Bradeuton, FL

Flight Never Took So Long

For K.A.B. 3

She was a long time coming
The constellation of her knees, hands, eyes
as high as any heaven
unreachable except by virtue
of her judgement

Child of the earth I
was a mere reflection of her stars
I could sow nothing in her mouth
she caught no scent of me—
buds lay molten, unmolded in my core

Still my sphere turns and tumbles
in her space
ellipsing sometimes closer, sometimes
farther from her brilliant parts

How desperately I know the Earth
wishes to send her spirit
far from her crusted body
to end her monotonous journey
and plunge willingly into the
blinding sight of the Sun
  As do I wish foolishly
  to throw myself
  before you, against you, inside you

Morris A. Kalmus
Philadelphia, PA

The Rubble Pile

The rubble pile like massive tomes
On shelves in ivy halls
Have epic tales that match times past.

In the upright hovels,
Now a rubble pile,
Where tales of loves lost and won
Are full of tears and joy
With deeds of heroes in war and peace, and
The conquerors of adversity
Who sailed wide oceans
To a strange new land
Beckoned by an iron lady
With torch in hand.

Come forward scribe and bard.
Descend the high towered nook.
Dig from the rubble.
Write pages of tales and songs
Found in the rubble pile
Yearning to be told and heard
Of broken hearts and scoring wins
And those with brawn and skilled
        bare hands layed brick and stone
For arcs and towers
Grander than in Rome and Babylon.

Maggi H. Meyer
Berkeley, CA

Square Within The Square

if i am blind and you follow me,
we may both fall in the ditch.

> before we do,
> you must view the city square
> with its crenellated church. . .
>> smell the breads and cheeses,
>> the "real" french perfumes,
>> sip some wine,
>> jostle and be jostled
>> in drygoods
>> buy a bit of lace,
>> recoil from sounds blaring
>> from disco shops.

above all, sense the people.

> everything is deliberate.
> even the faceless clock.

Fran Barst
NYC, NY

Shutter

I do not watch
the horses
running across the field
their auburn hair
burning in green
the mountains hunched over
their arched backs
as they run for
the setting sun

And the pigs
covered in brown matted hair
Snorting out mud
behind wooden fences
I do not watch them
choking on corn cobs
and later when their stomachs are slit
I will not see these hard kernels
drop like gun pellets
to cover the ground in their blood

I see the emerald lake
It is dark and thick green
like the liquid of an eye
and when one travels on it
it is like sinking
into an unknown time
in a plane with no propellors

My arms grow like seaweed
to gather mass
to be spit up by the water
but I cannot get out

Once I watched a mirror erupt
like so many tiny waves of silver
again like the sea
or the liquid of an eye
as a deer's brain splattered
in the distance

I buried that mirror
in a black mourning cloth
There is a dream
that spirits walk
from my world to yours
out of this place
If there is no light
they turn back
and crawl into their own darkness

I light no candles
The flowers on the shelves
have closed their lipped petals to kisses
and emit no fragrance
Their brittle stalks have dried
like cradled arms
with nothing to grasp
I have pulled down the shades
to keep out the moonlight

Nothing lives
Without
the touch of a finger
Without
the smoke of one's breath
in the cold

Babatunde Solarin
Euliss, TX

Moon Stories

The moon is full
And the Hyenas
Are laughing.
Grandma is waiting
With fire-baked cocoyams
And salted palm-oil.
Tonight,
We will learn
Of the Midget Ghost
Who lives in the Iroko tree.

Leave
The Fire-flies alone;
Grandma is waiting.

Deborah Dudley
San Diego, CA

A Linkage

I hardly knew him,
though knew him once,
and again,
across an unutterable year.
And new wings sprouted under our chins
where they flapped for stray
love
on bodies otherwise
slicked down, thinned,
with the passage over
of interminable convoys
hauling raw loneliness.

Not knowing what else to do,
we grappled,
strung each other out
on a long fish line,
catching little fish ideas
and waft of shore smells
from one dank recess
to where the other lay in his seaweed bed.
We spoke under water
like whales between oceans.

I knew only there were sparks
where he sat breathing.
He couldn't see them,
but were always igniting my carpet,
and up to hiss in my ear,
put smoke in my eyes.
So I gave in to enjoy the house
burning down;
pyromania written all over my face,
I said,
"Breathe again my dragon lover."

Mary Crescenzo Simons
Tulsa, OK

Loom In Essence

1. Waves of the weave

    A strange house
    a familiar breath
    a sanctuary
    in a secret room

    Cool breezes billow
    through a window
    where fibers
    ignite

    on a bed
    with waves
    of eloquent
    rhythms

    floating
    in an ocean
    of effortless
    concentration

2. Threads of the tide

    A strange house
    a familiar breath
    a sanctuary
    in a secret room

    Cool breezes
    through a window
    where fibers
    fray

Mary Crescenzo Simons
con't

on a bed
where waves
of eloquent
rhythms

are silent
in the ebb
of a dream
washed away

— ★ —

Ron Price
Philadelphia, PA

All Things Come

Snow is blowing through the gnarled
bough of an apple tree.
A white owl lites on one of the limbs.
The branches reach down
as though they were trying to climb
back into the earth.
A field mouse struggles across the snow.
The owl is sient.
He watches the mouse sink in drifts,
rise and continue
toward the tree where he waits.
There is no end
to the white plume of his patience.

Nita Penfold
Milton, MA

If I Were To Believe In A Male God

If I were to believe in a male God
He'd resemble my father: grey whiskers
grow sideways when He forgets they need trimming;
white hair curls to His neck in waves
so perfect I suspect setting lotion, hair clips;
above His ears, the edges try to take off
into horns, but He combs them down carefully.
The top of His head's a speckled egg, shiny,
freckled, with a few struggling survivors
left of the lush growth in old black
& white photographs of Him as a young man.

Like my father, God comes home
from His suit & tie speeches and His desk,
changes into worn jeans with a flannel shirt,
climbs the steep ladder and repairs the shingled roof.
Weekends, He knocks out walls and adds windows,
tinkers with lawn mower engines, refrigerator valves,
fixes clogged drains, recalcitrant ovens,
raises toasters from the dead. Neighbors stop by,
His children call long-distance for help
to change the washing machine belt,
or ask if He's got an extra television handy.

Above all, God would have to be a benevolent monarch,
all bluster; stomach a little large for His tall frame,
an overfondness for lemon meringue pie
and stolen spoonsful of Heavenly Hash.
Brown eyes twinkle as He provokes arguments
for their own sake. He chuckles over our little
disagreements, blushes over our indiscretions,
but would forgive us anything
to have all His children home eating at His table again.

Ann Chernow
Westport, CT

Patina

After a late December storm
When the snow stopped
And the air was cracking cold
We straddled the old wooden bench
Waiting for take-off
On our new silver skates
Ready to fly across the lake,
But not until the horses
Proved the ice to be
Sound.
We watched, leaning forward
As the team strained with the plow
Cutting swaths through the snow.
They reached center ice
Broke through, and
Disappeared.

— ★ —

Michael Joseph Phillips, Ph.D.
Bloomington, IN

Angie

Cute go go crafter,
Majestic dream hot goddess,
20th eon sensation !

Thomas Feeny
Raleigh, NC

Aftermath

over the rim
still the murky light
shadows cornfields
red dust hangs
in the long sky

in gullies, along
bone-dry streams
curl nests from which
all tiny life has fled

for months now
the air has shimmered with
burning on pond's
edge, where their journey
has led them
in silence the pair circle
a heap of rags, rubble,
shards of twisted metal

long into night
they weigh this random fusion
believing, disbelieving
come dawn, they resume
their trek

hope pitted against hope
that soon, again
reeds will tremble softly
sunlight startle
the frogs return

Jack Bernier
Morongo Valley, CA

Walking Mount Mitchell

Sing me the old songs
when sun warms flowering dogwood,
East Wind ruffles Q-tip feathery clouds,
cardinal flashes its plummage
like a great firebird winging
over verdurous greening fauna
while walking Mount Mitchell.
Listen to the wind talking
in the trees as scampering ground
creatures hastily take cover
under mulching leaves near roots
of deciduous and conifers.

Smokey rays of sunlight
piercing through the crown
of foliage warming a leaf
on a branch where a spider web
shines like tinsel thread
making an aerial bridge.
Footprints of bipedal wanderers
before me are etched
into the soil of life
where greening saplings
reach up drinking in light
filtering down from outer space.
Listen to the grinding, crunching,
melting down from glaciation
in the Pleistocene epoch
of geologic time and hearing a
pristine spring beginning.
This is walking Mount Mitchell.

Paul A. Query
Iowa City, IA

Hampton Beach

a sky of a secret color
sings of its lifelessness
in winds
of these. . .

reaches to grasp these
ornamented sands
in silver hands
which sift the fine grains
and wave them back down
left holding only colorful
writhing sacks

reaches to clutch these
weedless grasses
and laid-back trees
taut rigid by its steel fingers
in the utmost corner of the sky—
legs of a spider sun

reaches to touch these
leaf-veined eyelids
limestone lips
amidst deserts of skin
the outstretched beam
ends frustrated
half a hair away

Gary Waller
Pittsburgh, PA

How They Part In Novels

The good end happily, and the bad unhappily. That is what fiction means.

—Oscar Wilde

with the proper forms observed parting would occur
in some more comforting way we would recognize:
a public confrontation on a country house weekend
a contrived scene to establish tone and action
and consequences. One might have been surprised
with maid or madam, creating acts of passion
and despair. Like Masterpiece Theater.

or it could have been set in the Russia of your ancestry
wrapping ourselves ostentatiously in huge coats
then following unknowingly eager sled dogs
in opposite directions. Years later we return—
you with six children, husband, servants with their
pistols cocked, me with the awareness of what
I'd lost. A formal conversation with nothing to follow.
There might be dinner. Or drinks.
Anything to provide appropriate support
for the decorum the occasion required
Perhaps we would study the wine list and
wonder about the vintages we'd never taste.
It would be understood we would not
need to meet again.

there you sit and watch the telephone
here I cook an unnecessarily elaborate dinner

Paul J. Murphy
Bethesda, MD

Check

I was sitting at the counter in this diner last Friday night, having a cup of coffee and some bread pudding, when my waitress let out a yell and called to the owner who was working the register over by the door. "Those kids just ran out on their check!" she hollered, and the owner and the cook ran out after them, but returned in just a few seconds wet from the steady rain that'd been falling all evening, and announced that the culprits had gotten away. I almost ran out there with them because I'd been to the diner a few times and was beginning to think of myself as a regular, you know? I really wanted to help out if I could. But I didn't because I was afraid I'd just be a nuisance or that they'd take it the wrong way or something. What if they had caught the guys and wanted to rough them up a bit or just scare them and they couldn't because I was there and they didn't know what my reaction might be or how I might testify if the kids brought it to court and I was a material witness? Or if I got hurt while we were chasing them or if we caught them and there was a fight and I had my nose broken, who's to say I wouldn't sue the diner? Of course I wouldn't, but how could these guys have known that? If I had gone out there with them it would have been out of sympathy or some sense of what is right; nothing else. Oh, or what if they thought I was helping them out just so I might get the chance to crack some kid's skull on the sidewalk when all they wanted to do was get the money they were owed and maybe warn the kids to never come back? I mean they didn't know me that well.

But so anyway I didn't go out there with them and it really didn't matter after all because there was nothing to be done. The poor waitress, though; she was really upset. Apparently the diner has this rule: if your customers skip on a check, it comes out of your pay. She knew it, too, and didn't question the rule or try to make up some flimsy excuse. She wasn't even mad at the owner or anything for having such a rule, just at the scum who'd run out.

"Damn high school kids," I heard her saying. "Out driving their mothers' cars, with more money in their pockets than I make in a week. They got no right to run out like that. It's not even like they're hungry or anything; they're just getting their kicks."

I wanted to say something that would help her feel better, but I wasn't sure what. She might have thought I was trying to be sarcastic; I guess I was one of those high school kids myself not too long ago. Of course not anymore. It's true I'm doing pretty well for myself, but I think I know what it's like and how tough it must be to try and earn your living as a waitress. That was another thing: just because I'm making more money than she is, she might have thought I was patronizing her. She probably wouldn't have, because I don't think she's that kind of person, you know, but she might have, given the extraordinary circumstances. The thing is, though, I really wanted to help her. I even went so far as to eavesdrop a little on a conversation between the cook and the owner to find out her name. It's Carol. She's pretty good looking and all, with lots of black shoulder-length hair. She isn't petite or anything, but she isn't a monster. She's younger than the other waitresses; maybe twenty-five, twenty-six. and she has a wonderful smile when she looks right at you.

All of a sudden I got this crazy idea: why don't I pay for the check which the kids skipped out on? I figured the best way to help out Carol without appearing patronizing or sarcastic or looking like I was trying to pick her up or something, was just to pay for their check. There were four kids, and I figured it couldn't be more than about twenty bucks, and mine was only a dollar thirty-five. I had forty bucks on me, and some change. I thought maybe I'd just leave it with my tip, or better yet, ask the owner how much the kids' check had been when I walked up to pay my own. That way I could pay the owner and he would tell Carol after I'd left, and she'd wonder about me and be looking for me the next time I came in. Yeah. That was how I'd do it.

Then I remembered: I had a date the following night and no

way to get more money until my bank opened on Monday. Great. I
mean, maybe I could have paid for the check and still had enough
for the date too, but I wasn't sure. I didn't want to cut it too close.
The funny thing is, I would much rather have given the twenty
bucks to Carol than spend it on this date, who I didn't much like to
begin with, but I had already committed myself. I felt pretty bad
because I really wanted to help out, you know, but I just couldn't
be certain that I'd have enough money.

By this time I was all finished and Carol brought my check and
asked how everything had been. I told her that it had been
delicious, and smiled. She lowered her eyes and smiled also as she
cleared my dishes.

When she had gone I glanced at my check. She had added it up
wrong. It was supposed to be a dollar thirty-five before tax, but she
had it as a dollar fifteen. I waited until she passed again, then said
goodnight. I tried to give her a look which said that I understood
how she felt about those kids skipping out on her and that I wished
I could help and that I thought she was pretty nice and all. She told
me to be careful driving home in the rain.

So I brought my check up to the owner at the register and said
that I thought it was added up wrong. I said that I thought I was
undercharged by twenty cents. He looked at it for a second and said
I sure was, and thanked me for pointing it out. I said it was no problem, and put the change from two dollars on the counter as
Carol's tip.

"Do me a favor," I said to the owner as I passed him again on
my way out. "Don't tell Carol she messed up on my check. She's
had a tough night as it is."

He nodded with a grin as I opened the door and stepped out into the rain.

Michelle M. Tokarczyk
NY, NY

Years Later

At a crib in a room
of blue and red clowns
I cried for the crib
cornered in my parents'
grey-chipped bedroom.
Their arms wanted
to rock out the world,
but in their arms
I felt a world
without
primary colors.

You did not mean
to catch me crying,
but you pressed your hands
to the spaces in my back.
Your shirt absorbed my tears.

I do not know
if your arms felt
the tension
of cracked plaster,
but your arms lulled
that world to sleep.

Craig Peter Standish
Orlando, FL

Musing On Old Age And The Meaning Then Of Words

When I become a stiff
thick fingered old man,
with my hair grown sparse
everywhere but on my brows,
and my nose and ears grown
twice their youthful width and length,
will I still give a damn about
the meaning of words,
and how to scatter them with purpose
on the harmless serenity of white paper?
Will I still consume time
writing songs that no voice sings but mine,
or pass the time in musing on the cat
that prowls the faintly glowing hearth?
Who knows but that too is a poem.
Let face it: I'm cursed with words!

Michael Joseph Phillips, Ph.D.
Bloomington, IN

Angie

Hot top smooch goddess,
Go go runway dream empress
Hit doll paragon !

Alfredo Quarto
Seattle, WA

My Moonrise Companion

(for Kerry of Wiseman's Ferry)

She sighs softly in sleep
    as I wake her. . .
    mold her breast in an empty hand.
I can feel her heart beat through
       the covers of skin-
    those many layers of her world
 I wish I could penetrate.
I lie awake
      shorn of sleep as the day
     was born from the womb.
 She still wears her dreams,
     cloaked warm with the night,
though, sun shines through
      the roof, beams bright patterns
          on the floor.
I coax once more. . .until
  her eyes slowly open,
 she emerges from dark waters
     struggling to find the surface
   of the pond she swims in,
    catches her breath
 at the sight of my close shores,
   goes down under again
  content to submerge.

Vera Lee Baker
Claremore, OK

Seven Crows At Dawn

Shattering their frozen caws
Against the silent tapestry of snow-patches and ice-puddles
Seven crows flew over this crowless town,
Cold dawn street lights peering
Through bare-branched tracery,
Steam vents wavering the roofs of neighbors' houses.

The sun rose, heavy with memory,
Spreading across the blue jay's call,
Teasing me back to walk old paths,
Brown years crunching beneath my feet.

At dawn this morning seven crows.
Tonight, the moonlight-frosted town sleeps, unheeding,
Encircled by black lace edges of the trees;
The old owl hoots his far-off epilogue —
Melodious monotone, dark and woods-deep.

Dennis J. Bohr
Louisville, KY

Sleepwalkers

Sing a song, a poem, a painting
for the morning light to come
Darkness hides in its own shadows unafraid
slinking around every corner
seeping into households afraid
under 60 watts or sweaty sheets
Some persist laughingly, guzzlingly oblivious
but what's the rush, the fire?
Time creeps at its own petty pace
slower, faster than remarkable
Blackness will have its way with you
invade your head, kill its inhabitants
send you home in a paper cup
for daylight's harshness
You'll see nothing though it's all there
layered at your feet
your stale breath escaping your pounding brain
throat choked by smoke and memories of 4 A.M.'s.

John J. Haining
Tacoma, WA

Litany For A Lost Warrior

You, Chief Joseph—named Nez Perce, pierced nose,
By the traders who came to ravage your hunting grounds—
Molded the missioners' god to your ancient tribal lore.
You lived in friendship until the settlers
And the gold seekers intruded upon your meadows,
Blue with the delicate windflower
And the flashing blossom of the camas lily;
Until a few of your hothead, whiskey-incited braves
Laid waste the white men's cabins, killed in vengeance
And plunged you into a war you did not want.

Driven by the blue-coated cavalry,
You fled through the mountain passes,
Leading the spotted Appaloosa ponies you had bred
For generations in the hills of the Palouse.
You picked your way over deadfalls, through thickets of briar.
You stayed a day's ride ahead of the pursuing officer
Whom you derided as "General Day After Tomorrow"
As you rested around your council fires.

Sorrowfully, you buried your dead—braves, women, children—
After a surprise attack on your camp at Lost Hole;
Turned the cavalry's strategy against him and escaped
To make your last battle among the Bear Paw mountains
Where, realizing the futility of continued warfare,
You stacked your arms in honorable surrender
And declared in a voice resonant with pride,
"From where the sun now stands,
I will fight no more forever."

John J. Haining
con't

The slack-skinned drums are silent now;
The war ponies stand, heads drooping,
Their lackluster eyes clouded in dejection.
No smoke rises from the hearths of your gabled lodges;
Their brush-matted walls rattle in the brittle wind.
And the ancient heaviness of death
Hangs in the air like the mists of morning.
For you have been herded into exile by the blue coats.
The shrill dogs of betrayal yapping at your heels,
And once proud, free,
You have been penned in by markings on a map;
And seemingly, in your heaviness of heart,
Deserted even by the pale sorrowing god with the pierced hands.

Carol Ellis
Iowa City, IA

Death

When mind grows
against the skull
from knowing what
is never known,
thought becomes bone
and shatters.

The moon sets pulling
the sun down with it
and there is nothing
except the brain
smelling of dark.

James H. Cash
Louisville, KY

The Waitress

Whit Bonder was not an especially brilliant student, but he was inventive. Perhaps schemer would be a better word than inventor.

Early in his college career he learned to dig out any book or treatise his professor had written in the past, no matter how insignificant. Then when his point average needed a jolt he merely wrote a term paper quoting the prof's book liberally and profusely and it never failed him.

Once he even invented a book written by the Dean of Women in which the dear lady had made some startling statements about the sexual exploits of females of higher intelligence and learning, like herself. He went so far as to make up cards and records for the index and catalog at the campus library and inserted them himself when he had a chance. Sneaking was another of his gifts.

The cards and records listed it as an extremely rare book. In fact, the library had the only known copy and each time the professor tried to to find the volume the records indicated it was checked out our being repaired or otherwise unavailable.

Whit quoted the book extensively in one of his works of genius, knowing it would thoroughly entertain the professor's fantasies and also knowing the timid little man would never have the nerve to approach the Dean of Women directly and check on its authenticity.

Whit got the grade he wanted, as usual. And as soon as the term was over and the semester hours were his, once and for all time, he sold the "discovery" and its operating instructions - along with a few copies of the "sexual fantasy" section from Playgirl Magazine - to one of the many students who always seemed to have plenty of money but no imagination.

The problem of the moment, however, was two-fold.

First, Whit had to compose a thesis for his degree in industrial psychology. It had to deal with the psychological aspects and stresses of some form of employment. Anything from assembly line worker to nuclear mathematician. Also, since Whit was going for the Master's program, it was necessary to produce a project of some kind which he must present before a group of industrial relations counselors.

Secondly, Whit Bonder's well had gone dry. The mine shaft had been worked out. His mind was a Sahara Desert of ideas. Dry.

The only sensible thing to do was go to the library and start thinking and researching. So Whit went to a small, dingy, red-neck topless bar.

It was the middle of the afternoon and he seemed to be the only customer in the place. He got a can of beer at the bar and found his way through the darkened room to a booth in the corner.

A neon Pabst Blue Ribbon sign on the wall a few feet over his head was the only light near his booth. He started to pitch his books and briefcase on the seat next to him, but he was afraid something would get lost in the dark, so he stacked them on the table.

He took a long drink of beer and leaned his head back against the plywood booth and tried to think.

Up at the bar, the middleaged woman who was back with the cash register when he came in, had now walked around front and was perched on a stool, waiting for another customer to come in. She seemed to be lost in the words of a George Jones record playing on the juke box.

A younger woman came out a door at the end of the bar and hesitated, apparently letting her eyes get accustomed to the dark. She was very slim, perhaps too slim in the hips to be really pretty, Whit thought. Her skin was so pale she seemed to almost glow in what little light there was. At first he thought she was completely naked until he realized the dark inverted pyramid on her front side was a G-string or bikini of some kind. But it subtracted nothing from the startling effect as she turned and walked straight toward him, past the multicolored lights of the big juke box.

"Hi!" she said and smiled at him.

"Hi, yourself."

"Get you anything else? Another beer?"

"No. . .uh. . .no. . ."

Whit, in his confusion, trying to think of something to say, held up his can of beer as if to show her it was still half full, then he turned the can up and gulped its contents and said "Yes. . .uh. . .yes. . ."

"Good. Wanna buy me a drink?"

"Well. . .uh. . .yeah, sure. What do you drink?"

"Depends on you. Wanna buy me a ten-dollar drink or a twenty-dollar drink?"

"Well. . .I. . .uh. . .only got about six or seven bucks. Couldn't you. . .?"

"Oh, what the hell. It's a slow time of the day and I wanna sit down. Gimme the five."

Whit was fumbling through his pockets and his hands came out with a five and two ones. She took six dollars out of his hand and he watched her glowing white figure walk toward the bar and past the multicolored lights of the juke box.

He was almost completely absorbed with watching the girl walk back and forth, and yet the problem of his project held its small black cloud in the back of his consiousness. Perhaps it was a lifetime of planning and scheming that prevented him from forgetting it under the circumstances and enjoying the moment.

A spark, in fact, began to glow somewhere in his head when it occurred to him that she was after all just doing a job. Job? He was supposed to be researching the psychological stresses of some particular job. Why not the job of a topless waitress? Surely she must have. . .

She was back.

She handed him the can of beer and sat down across from him. Her five-dollar drink was a short glass, overflowing with ice cubes and a pinkish liquid which he suspected was a mixture of Big Red and gingerale.

He was nearly hypnotized by her more than ample breasts which appeared to him like large eyes which, even though they moved about constantly, still seemed to stare back at him from across the table.

"My name is Nicki. What's yours?"

Bonder had to stammer a minute to remember his own name.

"Whit. Whit Bonder. Glad to meet you, Nicki."

"What brings you in here this time of day, Whit? What's that? Short for Whitney?"

"Yeah. I'm a student over at State. Supposed to be working on a project."

"I saw the books and the brief case and all. What kind of student are you? What are you studying?"

"Industrial Psychology. I'm. . ."

"Oh, you're gonna be a psychiatrist, huh? That's great."

"No, not exactly. You see a. . ."

She always seemed to interrupt him in mid sentence.

"Let me tell you, Doctor, sometimes I think I need to see a psychiatrist. You wouldn't believe some of the. . ."

As her voice trailed on and on without ever seeming to come to a period or paragraph, Whit reached into his briefcase as if looking for something. Actually he was turning on the small portable tape recorder and placing the microphone where it would pick up their voices.

"Well, Nicki," he said, "you just tell me about your problems on the job and maybe it will help me with my project. Okay?"

"Sure, Doc. I'd love to. And maybe you can help me too."

"I doubt that, but who knows?"

He considered telling her about the tape recorder, but decided against it. He wanted her to talk freely and not try to "perform" for the tape.

"Doctor," she said, seriously, as she settled back "Do you believe in Martians?"

"I beg your pardon?"

"Martians. You know. From Mars and places like that."

"Well, really, I hadn't definitely made up my mind. But if you. . ."

"How do you feel about cockroaches?"

"I had always kind of thought I was against them, but now that you bring it up. . ."

"Perhaps I'd better start at the beginning, Doctor. Do you have time?"

"Nothing but, at the moment. Please tell me in your own words from the beginning. . ."

"Well, Doctor, you see I am a kind of entertainer. You know what I mean? I also have to wait on tables sometimes. But I get to dance and wear funny costumes and stuff. And the customers really like it. And I get to meet some of the funniest and nicest men and they buy me all sorts of presents and stuff. You know what I mean?

"Well, also, since I'm a long way from home and all that, I feel like I ought to do nice things like my Mom always taught me so I'm a Sunday School teacher every Sunday. I never miss. You know what I mean?

"Are you writing this down, Doctor?"

"Writing? Oh, no, I. . ."

"Well anyway. One Sunday just before Christmas I and my Sunday School class went out to cut a Christmas Tree for the class room. It was a cool but sunny afternoon and we enjoyed just browsing through the woods, just like we were shopping for the best tree.

"Then all of a sudden I hear something go *psssst! Pssst!* Like somebody was trying to get my attention. You know what I mean? So I look around and there's nobody there. I heard it again. Still nobody. Then I saw this bug down on the ground under the tree. Just a plain cockroach it was, but it seemed to be waving a little antenna thing at me. I looked at it and then I realized it was making some kind of noise. I was scared stiff, I must tell you.

"Then I thought I heard it say something. So I listened real quiet like and sure enough it was trying to talk to me. It said, 'come closer earth thing i must communicate with you.' Just like that. Like a machine talking. No punctuation or anything.

"Well, I don't mind saying it's not every Christmas I have a conversation with a cockroach. Did I feel silly! But I looked around and no one was watching so I leaned over and said, 'Who are you? What do you want?'

"And it said 'i am from another planet i have come to visit what you call earth we have been monitoring your tv for years and that is why my built in computer can talk your language'

"And I said, 'But you're just a bug. How did you get here?' and it said 'we are just as surprised as you to find odd creatures like yourself surviving these many years we wonder how you do it we hear you even go into outer space our planet is only what you call bugs like myself we are immune to all the diseases you humans have to live with we have no flesh like you to worry about why have not the bugs taken over this planet'

"Well, I could of told him a thing or two about bugs after some of the flea bags I've stayed in. But I went on talking to him till he started getting frisky with me."

"Frisky?"

"Yeah, I said, "What is it you want to know?' and he said, still talking like a machine without no punctuation or grammar or anything, he said 'our planet is dying out because of underpopulation no new infant bugs are born because there is no desire to mate between male and female we learn from your tv there is much drive to mate on this planet we wish to watch you do mating and see what is great attraction you seem to be kind that has great attraction for men wanting to do mating will you let me watch you and male human do mating'

"Well, I let him have a piece of my mind. I told him in no uncertain terms I was a nice girl and I didn't appreciate such language! So then he asked me what we were doing and I said cutting down a tree.

"'what will you do with tree' he said, like that.

"So I explained that we come out in the woods, find the prettiest and healthiest tree and cut it down and take it inside and put colored ornaments and popcorn and electirc lights on it. 'what is this for' he asked. I said, 'We are celebrating Christmas' and he said 'what means christmas' and I said 'It is the day we made up to mean the birth date of a vey important one.'

"'was this one a great scientist' he asked, and I said, 'No he was the son of a carpenter's wife about two thousand years ago.' And he said 'was carpenter not the father' and I said, 'No, not exactly.' Well, I could see this might not make much sense to him so just as I was starting all over to explain it to him a dog came trotting along, kicked his leg up and peed all over him. All of a sudden his fuses or something started to blow and smoke started coming out and the last I saw he was wobbling off under a leaf or something."

"And this is the last you ever saw of him. . .er. . .it?'

"No, not really. The next time we were on an Easter egg hunt with the same class. Then I heard the same old psst psst and there he was, good as new. And his mind was still on the same thing. 'now will you do mating so i can leave this peculiar planet' he said. Boy did I let him have it for keeping his mind in the gutter! Then he got inquisitive again. 'are you till celebrating the birth of the carpenters wifes illegitimate child' and I said, 'No, this is Easter, when we take chicken eggs and color them wild colors and hide them for the kids to find. This holiday represents the sons death,' I said. And he said 'how did son8die' and I said 'He was killed by his own people' and he said 'son must have turned out bad if you celebrate his execution so soon' and I said 'No, no, he was a Angel!'

"He always just got me so confused when I tried to explain something to him, know what I mean? So he just sits there and his little transistors and antennas buzzed and he said 'angel' a couple of times and then he said 'so he was california baseball player for your gene autry human now i understand we have watch your tv many years and heard humans yell kill the bum at these games but we never see the execution i will return this information to my planet perhaps next time we can witness your mating ritual'

"And away he flew, just like that."

Whit wondered if it was possible for this girl to make up the whole story. He doubted it. But more important was trying to figure how he could use it. Could he document it some way?

"Was this the last time you saw him. . .it?"

"Yeah, I guess. I don't know, really. Everytime I see a bug crawling I wonder if its him again. Know what I mean?"

"Yes. You do have a problem."

But Whit wondered how he could relate a fear of interplanetary cockroaches to the profession of topless waitress.

He had to admit there was a certain amount of sound scientific basis here. Cockroaches, he knew, had been around for untold thousands of years and had thrived in spite of all of mankind's efforts to destroy them. Their body structure was certainly much more suited to withstand the rigors and stresses of outerspace travel than the flesh and bones and fluids of mammals, not to mention the weight advantage. And there was their completely unexplained ability to communicate with one another. But how could this girl know all those things?

"Nicki, do you think you could find him. . .it. . .again?"

"Bullshit! I wanna get rid of him, not meet with him."

"Why are you so anxious to avoid. . .him?"

"Well, for one thing, I'm getting married. Know what I mean?"

"No, not exactly. You mean your husband would be jealous?"

"He invented jealous and he's working on perfecting the model. But that ain't the main thing. With that damn bug running around somewhere, every time we go to bed I'm gonna wonder if I'm doin' it on network TV on Mars or something. Know what I mean?''

"I can see that might inhibit your *tatigkeit* somewhat. But. . .''

"What does that word mean? You think I'm kinky?''

"No, no! It's a German word that means. . .''

"Well, anyway, Doc, we're cuttin' out, changin' our names and nobody's gonna find us again, not even that damn bug. And if you don't have no more money to buy me another drink, I gotta get moving around. Know what I mean?''

"Sure. Sure," he said, deep in his own thoughts. He looked around the saloon and noticed the other woman still sitting on the stool in front of the bar, still playing the same George Jones record over and over.

"I'm the only customer in here, Nicki. Why do you have to go?''

"Rules is rules, Doc. I bet you don't let patients come in and shoot the shit for free, do you?''

"No, I guess I don't do that very often.''

Whit gathered his books, zipped up his brief case, and walked out into the blinding sunlight.

All the way back to his furnished room near the campus he tried to build something in his mind. He felt he was standing on the bank of a river with great ideas and possibilities flowing rapidly in front of him. If he could just figure out some way to dam it up and harness the power of it.

He pitched his books and briefcase on his small, cluttered desk and sat back in the chair, exhausted and confused.

He decided he would play the tape back from beginning to end a couple of times and see if he could think of a way to salvage something, make a start, or forget it and try another approach.

As the cassette tape ran rapidly through rewind he suddenly saw a wisp of smoke coming from the little plastic vent hole in the recorder. He immediately grabbed the machine and stabbed his finger for the "stop" and "eject" buttons but it was too late. The tape was smoldering and when he tried to pick it up it was so hot he had to drop it. At the same instant a large cockroach ran out of the open briefcase and darted across the cluttered desk.

He slapped at it with a folded magazine and cursed the filthy, revolting creature but it disappeared over the edge, down the table leg and through a crack at the floor.

— ★ —

M.S. Childs
Northampton, MA

From Out Of The Pitcher

There are telephones flying awkwardly
and crashing at her marble feet. He
is holding out an empty water-tumbler;
the fountain is on fire. In the flames she

pours forever the pros and cons of her loves
and watches his hair singe. He can't believe
his mouth - she is in a chimerical heat, her back
glowing. Air is feeding the dance

of their distance. An impossible soot
is covering his eyelids and caking
on his cheek bones. Her eyes never leave.

Ellen Ziegler
New City, NY

Dry Browning

Outside the window
of the Home,
Autumn leaves are
their richest colors
before they fall.
Their grounded peers
rest in quiet,
burnished piles.
A gust passes,
sweeping them into
a fiery swirl.
The last one, rebel-red,
floats gently down,
on a heap set
to dry-browning.

My father sits inside.
Brown eyes glower
under wispy white eyebrows.
Their light is drawn
from inner shapshots.
His precious, antique head
rests on his chest mantle.
Against bright, corridor wallpaper,
the gray of him rests.
Alive for a moment, his eyes
reflect the splendor of his experience.
They lift me, as he once did,
high above those Autumn heaps
set to dry-browning.

Linda Quinlan
Madison, WI

Faz

In a hotel room
as quick as the phone call
I never returned
you were found lying face down
on a pillow
as if you were pushing through
to your mother then dead four years.

When I see kids hanging on the corner
we are there, together, sitting on concrete
with the taste of orange peels
and picking out the suckers
who stayed in high school.

I use to hide you
behind the counter of Ralph's Pizza,
begind his flower-covered apron
with the silly face painted on,
and shrug my shoulders
when your mother asked your wherabouts.

Faz, I am living away from Ralph's strong arms
that lifted us chair and all to the street
as a joke,
making our black nylons tear
against the metal legs.
We patched the runs
with fingernail polish
that dried hard,
hard as the stain I've put on myself
for thinking it was "getting out"
to "leave behind."

Victoria Amador
Denver, CO

My Daughter Sleeps In Snow

My daughter's white bed yawns a snowy welcome,
invites her: "Jump in! The feathers are fine
as your short yellow hair." My own blonde hair
wisps with restlessness these afternoons.
My daughter lifts her arms, lifts up *en pointe*
on her bare toes, floats into sunny air,
circles the sheets awhile, seeking a landing
place of downy pillows, then dives into sleep.

I watch her enviously these afternoons,
wishing I too could sink into cool comforters,
my yellow hair gleaming like new gold in
the sun. I hide her small face, my small face,
beneath the quilts I've sewn myself for her
and lie sleeples beside her as she dreams.

Lois H. Young
Philadelphia, PA

Seasoning

he loves me without license
crime his incentive
shoplifting for excitement
I wish the weather would change
and we were making love again
if my heart were stronger
he would be twenty years younger
his arms taut with pulling muscles
legs slightly bowed from the weight
of my body pressed into his

once I juggled four lovers
held them at a distance
now his proximity is sharp
yes, it is love I feel
I am not depending on false gods
to seal this lover's fate
I would rather be wife
than legally not belong
I remember when I wifed I seem
to forget those nagging responsibilities

but I have all the tasks
none of the rewards
if I were his wife I would be
protected on the outside
vulnerable on the inside, where
pain is more acute
red is my lust
white is my lost innocence
blue is my loyalty
glory waves around the onus
of legitimacy in March breezes
and when the weather changes
sun will warm my courage

ORDER BLANK

Your Name:_____

Your address:_____

With city, state and zip:_____

☐ I intend to submit for the 1987 number. I will submit
by_____(date). In a letter, tell us what to expect.
☐ *1984 Dan River Anthology All gone*
☐ *1985 Dan River Anthology* $ 9.95 paperback.
☐ *1985 Dan River Anthology* $15.95 hardcover.
☐ *1986 Dan River Anthology* $ 9.95 paperback.
☐ *1986 Dan River Anthology* $15.95 hardcover.
● ●

xx

_____*(D037-9) 1984 DRA,*   *Sold Out*

_____*(D039-5) 1985 DRA, paperback @ 9.95*   _____

_____*(D040-9) 1985 DRA, cloth @$15.95*   _____

_____*(D045-x) 1986 DRA, paperback @ 9.95*   _____

_____*(D046-8) 1986 DRA, cloth @$15.95*   _____

_____*(D060-3) 1987 DRA, paperback @ 9.95*   _____

_____*(D061-1) 1987 DRA, cloth @$15.95*   _____

Total for books   _____

*Multiple copy discount is 2% per book after the first. Multiply the number of
books ordered by 2, that answer is the percent of discount on your order. One
book gets no discount. 50% for 25 or more is the maximum.*
Amt. of discount   _____

Net for books   _____
5% Maine sales tax for all books going to **ME address**   _____
Ship: 1st book, $1.25. next 5, .50 ea. all over 6, .20 ea.   _____

Total for books, tax & shipping   _____

*(I know that some people find both the shipping and discount schedule to be a bit
complicated, but it is an attempt to be as fair as possible. Most publishers charge 3
to 5 times more for shipping than we do and give discounts only to bookstores. We
give the same discount to bookstores as to anyone else. Fairness, we call it.)*

Make checks payable to Dan River Press. Send to Order Department, PO Box 123, South Thomaston, Maine 04858 U.S.A.